TRUE CONFECTIONS

AN AMISH CUPCAKE COZY MYSTERY

RUTH HARTZLER

ROMANCE BOOKS

True Confections: An Amish Cupcake Cozy Mystery
(Amish Cupcake Cozy Mystery Book 1)
Ruth Hartzler
Copyright © 2019 Ruth Hartzler
All Rights Reserved
ISBN 9781925674941

PROLOGUE

Middle age was never so much fun - if you don't count the murders.

When her husband of thirty years runs off with a college student named Cherri, Jane Delight returns to Pennsylvania to work in her Amish sister's cupcake store. Having lost everything in the divorce, Jane now finds herself sharing an apartment with two feisty octogenarians and their quirky cat. Mr. Crumbles.

But there is no time to despair. A man is murdered in the cupcake store, and now Jane is the prime suspect. Enter brooding detective Damon McCloud, a Scot with a tragic past and a desire for justice.

Can Jane solve the murder, wrangle her new roommates, and stop herself from falling for the detective?

Or will she never get her new life on track?

True Confections is the first book in this delightful USA Today Bestselling series.

CHAPTER 1

"Jane Delight, have you heard a word I said?"

I stared at my husband blankly. He always said my full name when I irritated him. I couldn't quite take in his words. Maybe I was dreaming? It all seemed so surreal.

It was my fiftieth birthday and my husband had taken me out for dinner. He said he had news and I had thought he was going to invite me to renew our vows.

I looked around the restaurant. It was a trendy, expensive French restaurant, and my husband had not taken me to a fancy restaurant in years. In fact, we hadn't eaten dinner together in ages. He was

RUTH HARTZLER

always home late or away on extensive business trips.

"I can see you're upset, Jane," he continued.

I finally found my voice. "Upset? Upset?" I repeated. I heard my voice come out as a squeak.

"Now don't make a public scene, Jane," Ted said after tut-tutting. "I told you this in public so you wouldn't make a scene."

I had never made a scene. In fact, I was painfully aware I was a meek people-pleaser, and I continually vowed to overturn that tendency somehow.

"Is this some sort of a joke?" I asked hopefully.

His eyebrows knit in the middle. "How could you think I would joke about such a thing?" he said in a scolding tone. "No, we are getting a divorce."

I clutched my chest. "Don't I have any say in it?"

"It won't help to be clingy, Jane. We're getting a divorce, and that's final." He hesitated and then added, "I'm going to marry my mistress."

The waiter who had just arrived at our table turned red and hurried away. I was speechless, and that seemed to embolden Ted, as he pushed on. "I'm in love with her. I'm in love with Cherri."

"Cherry?" I repeated. "Did you say her name was Cherry?"

"Cherri with an i," he said, as if that explained everything. "She's having a baby. *We're* having a baby."

I dug my fingernails into the tablecloth. I had never had a baby. Ted had told me after we married that he didn't want children. I stared at him and realized my jaw was hanging open.

"Why didn't you tell me?" I asked, doing my best not to cry.

"That's the whole point of having a mistress," he said with a shake of his head. "Husbands don't usually admit it to their wives, but now I have to tell you because, well you know, because of the baby. Cherri is five months along."

"Five months?" I shrieked. "Your affair has been going for five months?"

Ted shook his head. "No, it's been going on longer than that. Now I know you signed a pre-nup when you married me, with me being a highly successful lawyer and all, but I wanted to give you some money because I feel bad."

I tried to say something cutting, but couldn't find my voice.

Ted pushed on. "Yes, I'd like to give you some

money, but I won't be able to. I'm sure you can understand that, what with the baby coming. I have to support Cherri and the baby, so I won't be able to give you any money after all. And I need the house."

"The house?" I repeated. "*Our* house?"

"It's a big house and there's only one of you, so you don't need a big house. I'm sure Cherri and I will have several children since she's only in her early twenties. You could go back to being Amish," he said with a dismissive wave of his hand. "After all, you were brought up Amish. You can go back to being Amish, and you won't need any money. Don't they live off the land or something? No electricity and all that. Think of the money you'll save."

"I can't go back to being Amish," I snapped. "I left the Amish when I was sixteen." The room spun and I feared I might faint.

He shrugged one shoulder and checked his phone. He shot off a quick text and put the phone back in his pocket. "What about your twin sister, Rebecca?"

"What about her?" I said through clenched teeth.

"She's still Amish."

I shook my head. "I don't understand what you mean."

"You can go and live with her. It's in another state, so we won't run into each other. I'm sure you don't want to happen across Cherri. It would be embarrassing for you."

I stared at Ted in disbelief. We had been married for almost thirty years and yet he was ending our marriage so easily. My head was spinning.

"But I have no skills, no qualifications. How will I find work?"

"You do have a degree in PR. You used to have a top job working for that fashion designer in New York. That's what you were doing when we met. You'll be all right. You'll soon make money again."

"Ted, that was almost thirty years ago," I protested, "and I was only an intern. I haven't worked in decades. No one is going to employ me now."

"You can live with your sister's family and babysit some kids or something," he said. "Go back to the Amish—you'll fit right in."

I sat there, frozen to the spot in disbelief. How could he do this to me? Sure, the spark had gone out of our marriage years ago, but I thought that was just the way it went with marriages. I had done everything I could to make the home a happy one, and I had thought Ted was content. Come to think of it, he had been far more content in the last few months, and now I knew why.

Something occurred to me. "Why are you doing this on my birthday? It's my birthday."

"You already said that once," he said. "Sure, I know it's not the ideal time to tell you, but then again I'm sure there is never a good time to tell you my mistress and I are having a baby and that you and I are getting a divorce. I suppose this is as good a time as any."

I looked at his face and wondered if I could upturn a plate of food over his head. Still, I had been brought up Amish, and that wasn't the thing to do. I couldn't even call Rebecca and cry on her shoulder. As she was Amish, she didn't have a phone in her house and of course didn't own a cell phone. She owned a cupcake store, and there was a phone there for the business, but I had to wait until working hours to tell her what had happened.

"This will be good for you," Ted said.

"Exactly how will it be good for me?" I snapped.

"Don't raise your voice, Jane. It will be good for you because you can get on with your new life."

My emotions had run the full gamut, from disbelief to remorse, to anger, to shock, and now I was angry once more.

I clutched the butter knife with both hands and shut my eyes tightly, thinking of all the horrible things I could do to Ted, and then sent up a silent prayer for forgiveness. When I opened my eyes, Ted was gone.

CHAPTER 2

Six Months Later

I had settled into the apartment over my sister's cupcake store. Compared to my former house, it was small, but at least I had the company of my sister through the day in working hours. She lived an hour's buggy drive from her store with her husband on their farm, so at night I was left alone with my thoughts.

I helped my sister with the cupcake store through the day and did a considerable amount of the baking. It had turned out to be a blessing that her previous assistant had left the day of my fiftieth birthday, and it seemed to me a small irony that her assistant had left to get married.

Rebecca and I had stayed close since I'd left the Amish after my *rumspringa* at the age of sixteen. I was happy for the company, but after six months, the situation with Ted was still raw. I told myself I had come to terms with it, but I wasn't quite managing, to be honest.

My sister's voice broke me from my reverie. "Jane, are you all right?"

I looked across the dinner table to Rebecca and her husband. Ephraim at once picked up his fork, but Rebecca continued to stare at me. "I thought you'd fallen asleep."

I chuckled. "How did you know I wasn't saying a particularly long silent prayer?"

Rebecca shook her head. "I've been around some particularly long silent prayers, and yours would have been the longest."

I continued to chuckle. The Amish said a silent prayer before, and usually after, every meal. As a child, it had been suggested to me to recite the Lord's Prayer, but I had never actually asked anyone what they said in their silent prayer. Still, when I was at an Amish meal, everyone opened their eyes just as I did and as I always silently recited the Lord's Prayer, I figured that's what they were doing too.

"Are you worried about meeting your roommates?"

I shrugged one shoulder and inhaled the heavenly scent of roasted chicken, mashed potato, and chicken gravy in front of me alongside the home-made applesauce, bread, and pickled cabbage. "Since I've lived in the apartment alone for so long, I *am* a little worried about how I'll fit in with roommates. The only person I've ever lived with was my husband." I quickly amended it to, "My *ex*-husband."

I scowled, but then realized the Amish don't hold grudges, so I plastered what I hoped was a peaceable look on my face.

"Eleanor and Matilda are lovely ladies," Rebecca said. "Anyway, you'll meet them tomorrow. They're very nice. Isn't that right, Ephraim?"

Ephraim simply nodded and piled mashed potato into his mouth. A kindly man, Ephraim wasn't one for conversation. He enjoyed working on the farm in solitude. Rebecca was more of a people person and since her children had grown up and gone on to have families of their own, I'm sure she enjoyed the interaction with people that her cupcake store brought her.

How I envied her life. Maybe if I had stayed

Amish, I would have a husband and children, even grandchildren of my own, just like Rebecca had.

I shook my head. I wasn't Amish, and there was no way I ever could be again. I could not live without electricity or internet, or even the Hallmark channel. Still, at times, I did envy the Amish ways.

"Those two ladies have been away on an awfully long cruise," I said to Rebecca. "I thought cruises were only for a few weeks, but they've been gone more than six months."

"Well, they're not your usual sort of people," Rebecca said, and Ephraim smothered a laugh.

I looked my twin sister straight in the eye. "What aren't you telling me, Rebecca?"

Her face was a picture of innocence. "Nothing, really. They're awfully nice, like I said. They're just a little unusual, that's all."

My mind ran through the possibilities. "When you say unusual, what exactly do you mean?"

She hesitated. "Matilda watches a television show all the time and always talks about it. I believe it's some sort of a mystery or detective show."

"What's the name of it?" I asked her.

She pursed her lips. "I can't remember, but I'm sure it's about an elderly lady who solves crimes."

I quirked one eyebrow. "Miss Marple?"

"It could be. That does sound familiar."

I was sure there had to be more to it. "So, is there anything else strange about them, Rebecca?"

"Not really. They're very spritely for English ladies in their eighties."

I knew when Rebecca said 'English' she didn't mean they were British; rather, that was her way of saying Eleanor and Matilda were not Amish. "You didn't tell me they were in their eighties," I said, trying not to sound accusatory. I imagined frail old ladies who needed considerable assistance in their daily lives. And how on earth would they make it up the stairs to the apartment? The stairs were quite steep.

"You wouldn't think it to look at them," Rebecca continued, "considering they don't do any hard work on a farm to make them fit. Anyway, to answer your original question about why they were away so long, they were on a world tour. I expected them back well before now, but they ended up staying in the south of France. They have sent me lots of letters. There's nothing to be nervous about. You'll like them, won't she, Ephraim?"

Ephraim nodded but did not look up from his pickled cabbage.

"Is that all that's worrying you?" my sister asked me.

I shook my head. "I was worried because that man was in again today."

That got Ephraim's attention. He set down his fork. "Colin Greaves?" His tone was grim.

Rebecca nodded.

"Did he give you any trouble?" Ephraim asked her.

"Just the usual," Rebecca said. "I'm sure he thinks if he pressures me enough, I'll sell him the bakery."

"He's quite unpleasant, but his manner falls just short of threatening," I added. "It's just as well that the other store not far from yours is holding out as well. It would be far worse if you were the last one left."

"I'm quite concerned about this," Ephraim said. "Maybe I should speak to the bishop about it again."

"There is nothing the bishop can do about it," Rebecca said. "The bishop is hardly likely to speak to Mr. Greaves and tell him to stop pressuring me."

"Then how will this end?" Ephraim asked her. "This Colin Greaves will continue to pressure you until you sell, and if those other people sell, then he'll be even worse as Jane pointed out."

"I'm sure he'll soon realize I won't give in to his demands and he'll decide to buy somewhere else, another parcel of property to develop," Rebecca said. Her tone was light, but I could see she was concerned.

"We could always sell the store and the apartment and buy somewhere else," Ephraim said.

Rebecca pointed to me. "What about Jane? And Eleanor and Matilda?"

"Don't worry on my account," I said. "And if you're worried about the other two ladies then I'm sure we could all find somewhere to rent together."

Rebecca shook her head. "*Nee*, I will not cave in and agree to sell the property to that man. He's just a bully and I'm sure he'll give up soon."

Ephraim and I exchanged glances. I didn't share Rebecca's opinion and it was clear to me that Ephraim did not either.

"Jane, last time we had dinner, you said you thought you were being followed but weren't too sure. Do you still think you're being followed?" Ephraim asked me.

"I don't know. Sometimes I think it's my

imagination, as I've only caught glimpses of whoever it is. I can't imagine why anyone would follow me."

"What about your ex-husband? Would he have you followed?"

"I've thought about that," I admitted. "I can't see why he would. He'd have nothing to gain."

Rebecca stood up abruptly. "I'll fetch the ice cream."

I stood up too, but she waved me down. "You sit there, Jane." With a backward glance over her shoulder, she hurried out of the room. I figured she was worried about Colin Greaves and wanted some time alone. The man was obnoxious, and in the time I had been working in Rebecca's store I had met him on several occasions. He had put on a charming front, but there was venom behind the smile. Colin Greaves had never actually threatened Rebecca, but I didn't know what would happen if she continued to refuse his offers to buy. Lately, his visits had been more frequent.

I wished there was something I could do to help, but I was practically penniless. Rebecca wasn't charging me much rent, partly to do me a favor and partly as Eleanor and Matilda paid well for the apartment. I had managed to save a small amount, but certainly nothing to help her relocate. Still, I knew Ephraim and Rebecca could afford to sell and then buy elsewhere, but Rebecca obviously did not want to do so.

Rebecca presently returned with ice cream and Shoo-fly pie. I had certainly missed Shoo-fly pie in my time away from the Amish, the delicious combination of molasses and brown sugar with a layer of cream on top. I preferred the wet bottom pie to the dry bottom, as I didn't like too much bottom crust. It certainly satisfied my sweet tooth. I had made it for myself over the years and make Shoo-fly pie cupcakes for the store, but nothing was ever as good as Rebecca's pies.

I selected a salty pretzel to eat with my ice cream, something else I had continued to do since I left the Amish. "I hope Eleanor and Matilda won't mind me living with them," I said to Rebecca.

She waved one hand in dismissal. "No, they're thrilled about it. When I first asked them if you could, they were both delighted, and they can't wait to meet you. They tend to bicker so it will be good for them to have someone else around."

I wiped my sweaty palms on my jeans. Why was I so worried about meeting these ladies? I supposed I had become a little set in my ways. On the other hand, I had been dreadfully lonely, almost thirty years of living with someone and then suddenly all alone. It would be good to have the company of others, no matter how quirky they were. Still, I wondered if there was something Rebecca wasn't telling me.

CHAPTER 3

I was in the kitchen making frosting for a batch of red velvet cupcakes when I heard a man's voice. The voice was familiar, and I soon realized it was that of Colin Greaves. I wiped my hands on my apron and in one move took it off and flung it on a nearby stool before hurrying into the store.

Rebecca's face was white and drawn. Greaves was smiling that thin-lipped smile he always offered. Waves of citrus, vanilla, and vetiver emanated from him. He always wore a slathering of the same male cologne, and it was overpowering. While I wasn't allergic to perfumes or colognes, too much of a strong scent always gave me a sinus headache.

"Mrs. Delight," he said with a slight nod before turning his attention back to Rebecca. "I'm prepared to increase my offer, but it's for a limited time only. A limited time," he repeated, as his eye twitched and he rubbed his mouth.

Rebecca and I exchanged glances. "It doesn't matter how much you offer, as I'll never sell to you," she said ever so politely. I admired her patience.

Greaves folded his arms over his chest. "And what does your husband have to say about it? I *am* aware the property is owned by both of you."

I chose that moment to interrupt. "Ephraim certainly doesn't want to sell. I wouldn't risk annoying him by going to speak with him."

Greaves sneered at me. "Well, I might take that straight from the horse's mouth. I'll pop over this afternoon to have a chat." He took a tissue from his pocket and wiped his brow.

I knew Ephraim would refuse to sell. Greaves was still speaking. "Mrs. Yoder, I know you don't want to give up your cupcake store, but you won't have to as such. With the amount of money I'm offering you, you could buy another store and apartment in a nicer and far safer place of town. It's a good business decision for you."

Rebecca put her hands on her hips by way of response.

"Is there anything that would encourage you to sell?" Greaves asked her. He frowned and rubbed his mouth hard, a gesture I thought peculiar.

When Rebecca shook her head, he continued, "I should think you would like to move to a safer part of town. This area is older and it's no longer safe. Not safe at all." His lip curled as he spoke.

I took a few steps forward. "Are you threatening my sister?"

Greaves smirked at me. "Of course not. Whatever would give you such an idea?"

His tone chilled me to the bone. His words might have denied his threat, but his tone and attitude made it clear his words were, in fact, a warning.

"I think you should leave," I said in the firmest tone I could muster.

"I'll leave when I'm good and ready," he said with a snarl. "I'm glad these samples are catching on around town." He reached for the nearest cupcake and popped it into his mouth. Rebecca always had a tray of tiny cupcakes on the countertop for customers to sample.

I stood there, somewhat at a loss. I couldn't forcibly make the man leave, so I didn't know what to do. I figured we would just have to stand there awkwardly until he left. I fervently hoped customers would come in.

I wasn't wondering what to do for long. To my shock, Greaves made a strange, strangled sound and fell to the ground.

I hovered over him and loosened his tie, absently noting it was pink paisley silk, before signaling to my sister. "Rebecca, quick! Call 911."

"My heart," he muttered. All the color drained from his face and he broke into a heavy sweat.

"Do you have medication?" I asked urgently, and at once rifled through his coat pockets hoping to find a bottle of medication.

What happened next was a blur. Later I remembered the paramedics arriving, and Rebecca flipping the sign on the door to Closed.

One paramedic ushered us out of the room and into the kitchen, where we stood, clutching each other.

I did my best to listen in. I overheard the paramedics saying Greaves had a feeble, rapid pulse. I turned to my sister. "Did they say his blood pressure wasn't recordable? That's not possible, is it?"

"It's not good to eavesdrop," Rebecca scolded me.

I sighed and put my ear back to the door. "Ventricular tachycardia. I wonder what that is? They asked if he was taking anti-arrhythmic medications, but I couldn't hear his response."

"Do you think he had a heart attack?" Rebecca asked me.

I shrugged. "I don't have a clue, to be honest, but it does seem to be something to do with his heart."

"The poor man," Rebecca said. "I will pray for him."

I nodded but then stepped away from the door when I heard footsteps approaching.

"We're taking him to the hospital now," one of the paramedics said. "It's probably best if you don't go back into the store until the police come."

"The police?" I echoed. It was all so surreal. "Why would the police come when someone's had a heart attack?"

The paramedic hesitated and then said, "It doesn't appear to be a heart attack, and since we don't know exactly what it is, we called the police." With a nod at me, the paramedic left the room.

"I wonder what he meant?" Rebecca asked me.

Unlike my Amish and thus television-less sister, I watched a lot of crime shows on TV. I was fairly certain the paramedics thought Greaves had succumbed to foul play, and as he had not been shot or stabbed, I could only assume he had been poisoned.

I remembered he had eaten one of the sample cupcakes, but if he had been poisoned by that cupcake, then any one of our customers could have eaten it. I shuddered.

"What's wrong, Jane?" Rebecca asked me.

"I'm just a bit uneasy about it all," I said, not wanting to tell her that I suspected Greaves had been poisoned.

As I was considering precisely what I should tell Rebecca, a man's voice called out from inside the store.

Rebecca and I hurried out to find two uniformed officers. Both were men. The taller one introduced himself as Alex Albright and his partner as William Worth. Rebecca and I duly introduced ourselves and Officer Worth wrote our names in a notepad.

"So, what happened here this morning?" the taller officer asked.

"Mr. Greaves came in and offered me more money to sell my store to him and then he fell to the ground. I called 911."

I nodded while Rebecca was speaking.

"And did he eat anything or drink anything while he was in here?" Officer Albright asked.

I clutched my stomach. That meant they did suspect poison.

"He ate a cupcake from our sample tray," Rebecca said, indicating the tray.

"It was a chocolate one," I supplied.

"Bag these, Worth," the taller one said.

It was then I noticed Officer Worth was wearing gloves. I hadn't noticed if he was wearing them before. He carefully popped all the little cupcakes into a baggy.

"Did anyone else eat any of those cupcakes today?" Albright asked Rebecca.

"I think I noticed about five or so samples missing," Rebecca said.

"Did you actually see a customer eat any of the sample cupcakes this morning?" he asked her.

Rebecca nodded. "Yes, more than one customer."

"Could I have their names?"

Rebecca shook her head. "I don't know. Only one of them was a regular customer. Mrs. Bates."

"I don't suppose you have her address or any contact details?"

"As a matter of fact I do. She's a regular customer and every year she orders a birthday cake for her husband. Shall I fetch her contact details now?"

He nodded in the affirmative. Rebecca walked into the kitchen and I closed the gap to the officer. "I didn't want to say this in front of my sister, but do you think Mr. Greaves was poisoned?" I asked him.

"Sister?" he said with surprise. "But she's Amish and you're not."

"I left the Amish after my *rumspringa* at the age of sixteen," I said. "We're twin sisters actually. Identical twins."

His jaw fell open. "You look nothing alike!"

I didn't point out that we would indeed look alike if I wore Amish clothes or if Rebecca let her hair down from under her prayer *kapp*. *Lucky he's not a detective*, I thought unkindly.

The officer soon gathered his wits. "Why would

you think he was poisoned?" He regarded me with narrowed eyes.

"Because police don't get called to heart attacks," I said. "And you're taking away the sample cupcakes. You know they were out there for anyone to eat."

As the officer just made a grunting sound, my imagination ran away with me. Would my sister become a suspect in an attempted murder? After all, Greaves had threatened her. And while the cupcakes were out on the countertop for anyone to eat, the police could conclude my sister slipped a poisoned one on there for Greaves when he came into the store.

"So where do you live now?" the officer asked me.

I pointed to the ceiling. "I live in the apartment above the store," I told him. I took a deep breath and then added, "When my husband left me, my sister rented me the apartment above the store."

"I see, well we'll take both your statements when your sister returns with those contact details."

Just then Rebecca hurried back into the store and handed the officer a slip of paper. His partner had been on his cell phone for the last few minutes and I was alarmed to see him beckon to the other officer, a worried look on his face.

"Excuse me." Albright walked over to confer with Officer Worth.

I couldn't hear what they were saying, but it didn't look good. I suspected Mr. Greaves had passed away, and I also suspected that my sister might be the main suspect.

CHAPTER 4

The officers left after telling us that detectives would be along presently. I still hadn't told my sister that I thought Mr. Greaves had probably passed on. I couldn't quite come to terms with the fact that one of our cupcakes might have been poisoned, and my head was reeling with the implications. I turned to Rebecca. "What do we do now?"

She shrugged. "I suppose we just wait for the detectives. We could do more baking, but then again I don't know how long it will be before they let me reopen the store."

I thought back to all the crime shows I had seen on TV. "I'm pretty sure you'll be able to open again tomorrow morning." I was going to say more but was startled by a loud bang on the shop door. I thought it must have been the detective, but as I turned around I saw two women peeping through the glass. One was tall and stick thin, the other, shorter and on the plump side. The tall one was clutching something under her arm.

"Eleanor and Matilda!" Rebecca exclaimed with joy. She hurried over to the door and opened it.

The two ladies all but fell inside. Waves of rose-scented perfume preceded them. Matilda, the shorter one, embraced Rebecca in a tight hug, and Rebecca patted her awkwardly on her back.

I bit back a smile. After all, the Amish in my former community were not given to public displays of affection. Eleanor marched over to me and thrust something into my arms. It was only when it scratched me and jumped away I realized it was a cat.

Eleanor let out a shriek. "You scared him! The poor thing."

I clutched my head. Maybe I was having a nightmare after all. First of all, Mr. Greaves had threatened my sister and then had most likely passed away, and now my two roommates had arrived and one had thrust a cat at me.

Rebecca too looked flustered. "Eleanor and Matilda, this is my sister, Jane. Jane Delight."

Matilda chuckled. "Is that really your surname, Delight? Anyway, forgive my rudeness. I'm delighted to meet you." She burst into laughter. "I'm sorry, no pun intended," she added when she finally stopped laughing.

Eleanor was on her hands and knees, looking behind the shop counter. "Here kitty, kitty," she was saying. Suddenly she lunged forward. She disappeared from sight with a grunt and then stood up, clutching a terrified cat to her. "Hello, Jane. It's lovely to meet you. Sorry I yelled at you, but I was worried about Mr. Crumbles." She held up the cat as if I didn't know who Mr. Crumbles was.

Mr. Crumbles was gray with rough fur, patches of which were missing. His eyes were huge and orange. I was glad I could not see his teeth but imagined they were long, yellow, and needle-sharp.

"Matilda and Eleanor, we can't have a cat in the store. What about health regulations!" Rebecca said. "Let's go upstairs to your apartment."

"What if the detectives come while we're away?" I asked her.

"Detectives?" Eleanor and Matilda said in unison.

Rebecca waved to the back of the shop where the stairs to the apartment were. "Let's go upstairs and I'll explain everything." To me, she said, "They can ring the bell. I'm more worried about the health inspector finding a cat in my shop."

With that, we all hurried upstairs. To my surprise, Matilda and Eleanor took the steps two at a time. I didn't know what to tell them or where I should start. Should I say I hoped they didn't mind me living with them, or should I tell them what had happened to Mr. Greaves? Did they even know who Colin Greaves was in the first place?

Thankfully, Rebecca came straight to the point. "Do you remember a man by the name of Colin Greaves?"

Both sisters said that they didn't. "He owns the parking lot opposite my store." She pointed in the direction of the front window. "He's been buying up all the stores in this street. He wants to demolish them because he wants to build a mall here. He's bought them all except my store and the building owned by the health food and supplements shop. His demands have become more and more urgent."

"Did he threaten you?" Matilda asked.

"He made a veiled threat today," I said.

Matilda gasped. "Did you call the police?"

Rebecca hesitated, so I thought I should continue the explanation. "Right after he threatened Rebecca, he ate one of the sample cupcakes. You know, the ones Rebecca always has on the countertop? Anyway, he fell down and dropped dead."

Rebecca's hand flew to her throat. "Dead? Did you say dead?"

I instantly regretted being so forthright. "Well um, not exactly. I'm not too sure," I sputtered, "but I think he might have passed on after the paramedics took him away."

Rebecca had turned as white as a sheet. "What makes you think that?"

I felt bad for upsetting her. "It's the way the officers were whispering to each other after Officer Worth took the call. I mean, Mr. Greaves might be all right, but I'd be surprised if he hadn't been murdered."

Matilda tapped her chin. "And if the police knew he threatened you, then you would likely be a suspect in his murder, Rebecca."

Rebecca sat with a thump on the nearest overstuffed chair. "Surely not?"

Eleanor had remained silent, and now spoke. "We found a stray cat on the way home. Obviously, he was not owned by anyone. I named him Mr. Crumbles. It suits him, don't you think?" She held him out for us to inspect, but he wriggled and tried to claw her. In fact, he managed to do so, and one long strip of blood appeared on her arm. "The poor little thing. He's scared," Eleanor said, clutching the struggling cat to her chest.

Mr. Crumbles managed to free one paw and swiped at me, so I took a step backward.

Matilda rolled her eyes. "There are more pressing matters than a stray cat, Eleanor," she said in a scolding tone. "You don't want our landlady to go to prison for life, now do you?"

Rebecca wrung her hands and twisted them in her apron.

"I'm sure it won't come to that," I said in soothing tones.

Matilda apparently came to her senses. "No, of course not. I'm very good at solving crimes. I've seen every episode of *Miss Marple* in the newer television series. Both actresses, mind you. And I've seen the older series too, but I don't like it as much. I've read every book Agatha Christie ever wrote. I'm sure I will be quite good at solving this murder." She smiled widely as she said it.

Eleanor interrupted once more. "Jane, you

certainly cleaned up the apartment nicely. We'd left it in rather a mess, I'm afraid."

"I hope you don't mind me staying with you?" I asked her.

Eleanor extracted one hand from the cat and waved it at me in dismissal. "Of course not, dear. There are three bedrooms and two bathrooms. There is more than enough room for the four of us."

It took me a moment to realize the cat made up the fourth.

"And don't worry about the little cat. We took him to the vet on the way here. He'll settle down when he realizes no one will hurt him. Matilda, do you have that cat food in your purse?"

Matilda reached into her purse, retrieved a small can of cat food, and threw it hard at Eleanor. It whizzed past my nose, and I ducked.

To my shock, Eleanor caught it with one hand. Her reflexes sure were good. "I'll just go and feed Mr. Crumbles," Eleanor said and disappeared from the room.

"Would you like me to make you some sweet tea, or maybe some coffee?" I asked Matilda. "And maybe some meadow tea for you, Rebecca?"

"I'll have coffee, please," Matilda said, "and

I'm sure Eleanor would like some too when she finishes with Mr. Crumbles. Maybe put some extra sugar in your sister's meadow tea. She's gone pale."

"I'm all right," Rebecca protested feebly.

I walked into the kitchen to make the meadow tea. "What a lovely coffee machine you have," Eleanor said. "Do you mind if Matilda and I use it as well?"

"Of course I don't mind. Help yourself to anything of mine," I said. "It's awfully good of you to allow me to live here too."

"Well, it helps with the rent to be honest," she said, "even though your sister doesn't really charge us much. Everything helps. A penny saved is a penny earned, don't you think?"

I nodded. It was then I realized she had rollers in her hair. I wondered why I hadn't noticed before, but I figured it was because the day had been quite a strange one. On a normal day, it would have been the first thing I noticed. "Would you like something for your arm?" I asked her.

She looked at her arm. "No, I've had worse. It's stopped bleeding now. Poor Mr. Crumbles. No doubt he's had a hard life living on the streets, but he's come to a good home." She narrowed her eyes and shot me a look of suspicion. "You do like cats, don't you?"

"I love cats," I said. "Rebecca and I had cats growing up. My husband was allergic to cats and dogs." After I said it, I wondered if it was true. In fact, I wondered if anything my ex-husband had told me was true.

I returned to the living room with two mugs and placed one in front of Rebecca and one in front of Matilda, then went back to the kitchen to fetch my cup and Eleanor's cup. Eleanor had already picked up Mr. Crumbles who had eaten his food in double quick time. He seemed calmer now and had stopped struggling.

"I've been watering your plants for you while you were away," I told them. "Rebecca was watering them until I moved in, and then I took over for her."

Both ladies thanked me. There was a small courtyard at the back of the building with a high walled fence. In it was a greenhouse filled with all manner of herbs and other plants. I didn't have much of a green thumb and was surprised they were all still alive, let alone thriving.

"After Mr. Crumbles settles in, we can let him into the courtyard while I watch him," Eleanor added. "I don't think he'll be able to scale those walls, and he will enjoy being outdoors."

The sound of a doorbell caused Rebecca to jump to her feet, nearly knocking over her meadow tea. "That must be the detectives!"

I hurried after her to the stairs.

The doorbell rang again twice more by the time Rebecca reached it. She flung open the door.

Standing outside the door was the most handsome man I had ever seen. Upon reflection, I figured others might not find him handsome, as he had a rather rugged, wearied look about him. Still, there was just something about him that got my heart racing. He was tall and well built, with hair that had been closely cropped and he had the bluest eyes I had ever seen.

"Mrs. Yoder? He consulted his notebook. "Mrs. Yoder, Mrs. Delight?" he said. His accent was Scottish. Then he bowed deeply.

CHAPTER 5

"*M*iss," was the first word out of my mouth. "Not Mrs. I'm divorced."

Why did I say such an obvious thing? I silently scolded myself. And why did he bow?

I did not have to wait too long to find out.

Matilda's voice rang out behind me. "Did you bow? Why did you bow?"

The slow red blush spread over the detective's handsome face. "I was bowing to the Amish ladies."

Did I hear him correctly? "There is only one Amish lady here," I told him. "I am not Amish."

He looked even more discomfited. "Forgive me. I thought you were an Amish lady too, although not in costume."

"Costume?" Rebecca said.

It was then I noticed the man standing next to him. His hair, what there was of it, was black, and he had the most outrageous combover. He was of indeterminable age, and had a rather stooped posture. His head reached the other detective's shoulder.

The handsome detective held up both hands in front of him. "Allow me to start from the beginning. I am Detective Damon McCloud, and I haven't been in these parts long."

"No kidding," Matilda muttered.

The other detective murmured something unintelligible, and then grunted, "Detective Carter Stirling."

"I am doing my best to be particularly courteous to the Amish people," Detective McCloud said. "There are no Amish people in Scotland."

I folded my arms over my chest. "Why did you think I was Amish?"

The detective did not meet my eyes but consulted his notes. "I had both your names. I was told you were twin sisters, so I assumed you were both Amish."

I nodded slowly. "I see." Maybe I needed to wear more make-up and think about buying some nicer clothes. I had let myself go ever since my husband had run away with a woman less than half my age. I felt a little guilty for being vain as I had been raised not to be vain, but I had spent most of my life in the non-Amish world where vanity was normal and everyday.

"And we haven't been introduced," Detective Stirling said in a pointed tone to Matilda.

"I'm Matilda Birtwistle, and my sister Eleanor and I have just arrived back in town after a world cruise. We have an alibi for the murder. You can check our flights, and then we were most likely at the vet not far from here at the precise moment the vic was murdered."

"The vic?" I repeated.

"Yes, the victim," she explained with a sigh. "The *vic*. Technical talk. The nice detectives here understand."

"And why did you say the man was murdered?" Detective Stirling asked.

"That's my fault," I admitted. "When the officers came, one of them took a call. After he whispered to the other officer, his manner changed so I figured that Mr. Greaves had passed away."

"I see."

I looked at him, waiting for confirmation or

denial or some sort of clarification, but there was none.

He pushed on. "I would like to speak with both you ladies, and then other officers will be along presently."

"Will my sister be able to open the store tomorrow?" I asked Detective McCloud.

"I don't see why not," he said, "but I will advise you of that later today. Miss Matilda, would you mind if I spoke with both these ladies in private?"

Matilda nodded and then walked out of the room. Her footsteps suddenly stopped, so I had no doubt she was eavesdropping. Detective Stirling hurried after her. That would certainly spoil her plans.

"Please tell me what happened in your own words," Detective McCloud said.

Rebecca looked at me, so I figured I had to be the one to do the talking. "Mr. Greaves came into the store today to ask my sister to sell. Rebecca always has cupcake samples on the counter. He ate a chocolate cupcake, and then soon afterwards clutched his throat and fell to the ground. Rebecca called 911 and I looked through his pockets for medication."

"Why did you think he had medication?" he asked me.

My hand flew to my mouth. "Oh, I forgot. He said, 'My heart,' so I thought he had a heart condition and might have some sort of pills, but I couldn't find any. The paramedics came quite soon and worked on him for a while. They told us they had called the police."

The detective nodded at Rebecca. He made to bow again but stopped himself. "So, do you have anything to add to that?"

Rebecca shook her head. "My sister thinks Mr. Greaves was poisoned…" she began, but the detective interrupted her.

He fixed me with a steely gaze. "Why would you say that?"

I did my best not to roll my eyes. "If he was murdered, he obviously wasn't stabbed or shot or hit over the head. I can't think of anything else that would have harmed him other than poison." The detective still looked suspicious, so I added, "And of course I know the police wouldn't be called unless there were suspicious circumstances."

He seemed somewhat mollified at that. "Quite so," he muttered.

Rebecca appeared agitated. "Mr. Greaves was

poisoned? Could there be other poisoned cupcakes in my store? I'm quite concerned. Some customers ate those samples today. In fact, one of my regular customers ate one of the samples earlier."

The detective consulted his notes. "A Mrs. Bates?"

Rebecca nodded.

"We've been in touch with her, and she is fine."

Rebecca breathed a sigh of relief.

"Did you notice anyone in the store before Mr. Greaves came in? Anyone acting suspiciously?" The detective held up one finger for emphasis. "Take your time, both of you, and think carefully before answering. This could be quite important. Please mention anything that occurs to you. Even if it seems a small and inconsequential detail to you, it could still be significant."

Rebecca and I exchanged glances. "I don't think anything out of the ordinary happened today," I said. "Well, apart from the murder, that is."

Rebecca readily agreed. "Otherwise, it did seem quite a normal day," she said. "We had some customers who were not regular customers, but of course that happens every day. There wasn't anyone who seemed to be acting suspiciously."

"Surely no one would have put a poisoned

cupcake on the sample tray in the hopes that Mr. Greaves and no one but Mr. Greaves would eat it," I said. "Mr. Greaves always comes here alone. How would anyone know he always ate a sample cupcake? Several other people ate the sample cupcakes today. Like my sister said, one of them was Mrs. Bates. As she's unaffected, it means not all the cupcakes could have been poisoned. It doesn't make sense."

The detective gave a slight nod but did not respond. It wasn't looking too good to me. The only way Mr. Greaves could have been poisoned with a sample cupcake was if someone put it there especially for him. No person could, apart from myself and Rebecca. It looked like both of us might be the prime suspects.

Something occurred to me. "If Mr. Greaves was poisoned, maybe he was poisoned before he came into the store today and it had nothing to do with the sample cupcake," I offered.

Before the detective could respond, Matilda re-emerged. "That's right!" she said. "It's very rare that a poison can act so quickly. Strychnine and arsenic in big enough doses are fatal quite soon after administration, as are botulinum and polonium, but there are not many poisons that work so quickly. Take thallium, for example. It would have to be a mighty big dose of thallium to kill someone quickly, and usually it's given over time. Maybe whatever killed Mr. Greaves was given to him over time."

The detective opened his mouth to say something, but Matilda thrust a card into his hand. "I've just fetched the vet's card from my purse. She can tell you the exact time I was there, which gives me a solid alibi. Oh, my sister Eleanor too. The other detective is looking through our apartment. I told him we had nothing to hide."

"Thank you for that," McCloud said. "You do seem to have rather a good knowledge of poisons for the average citizen."

"I've read every book Agatha Christie has ever written," she told him proudly. "Yes, I know quite a lot about poisons."

The detective's eyes widened, but he did not respond. Instead, he turned to me. "I'd like you and Mrs. Yoder to come downtown to give your witness statements as soon as you can. As Mrs. Yoder's store has to remain closed today, is it possible both you ladies could come to the station within the next hour or so?"

"Yes, I can drive my sister," I said.

He raised one eyebrow. "In a buggy?"

I shook my head. "I'm *not* Amish. I drive a car." I really did have to start wearing make-up again, and nicer clothes for that matter. Maybe I should even start going to the any-time gym nearby. I shook my head. No, that was going a little too far.

The detective handed me his card. As he did so, our fingers brushed for the briefest moment and a jolt of electricity ran through me. What was wrong with me? Why did I find this detective so attractive?

CHAPTER 6

"I've never been inside a police station before," Rebecca said in a small voice.

I wrinkled up my nose at the smell of stale coffee and pine disinfectant. "Don't worry. The detectives will simply ask you what happened."

"But I've already told the police twice," she lamented.

"That's just how police are," I told her. "You'll probably have to repeat it several times. I remember when Ted and I were burgled about five years ago, and we had to tell the police over and over again what had happened. Still, I was grateful because they caught the people who did it. They are only doing their job. There's nothing to worry about because we know we didn't do it."

Rebecca's fingernails dug into her over skirt. "But *somebody* did it," she said. "What if the poison was in my cupcake? What if there are other poisoned cupcakes in the store?"

"I don't think that's likely since the police have taken them all," I said.

Rebecca nodded slowly. "Oh yes, how could I have forgotten? We are going to be baking until late tonight. Not that I mind," she added hastily. "It only matters that everyone is safe. I wouldn't like anyone else harmed by my cupcakes."

I drew a deep breath and exhaled slowly. Rebecca and I were sitting on hard, blue plastic chairs in a large lobby, the walls of which were painted dark blue as well as various shades of cream and ivory. Behind us were several frosted windows in blue metal frames. Over to one side was a cream countertop behind which was a clearly bored officer tapping away at a computer. A big blue sign was on the wall, but without my glasses I couldn't read what it said.

I yawned and stuck my legs out in front of me. "You know, Rebecca, I really doubt the poison is in your cupcakes, but the police will know soon enough."

Rebecca held up both hands, palms upward. "But how will they know?

"Well, I imagine the medical examiner will examine the contents of Mr. Greaves's stomach and see if there are bits of poison cupcake or whether there was something else poisoned inside his stomach." As soon as I said it, I doubted my reasoning was correct. "Come to think of it, perhaps that isn't what they do. I really don't know how it works."

"We'll have to ask Wanda Hershberger to explain it to us," Rebecca said.

Now I was even more puzzled. "Who is Wanda Hershberger?"

"Do you remember the Hershbergers from your time here as a child?"

I did remember a kindly couple. "Oh yes, I do remember them. They were nice."

"Wanda is their daughter, and Wanda's daughter does filing for the medical examiner's office."

"Aha." I tucked it away for further notice in the recesses of my mind. It might prove useful.

"I wonder who did murder him?" Rebecca said.

I shrugged. "I'm sure he had a lot of enemies. He didn't seem the most ethical sort of person and he was very wealthy. That combination probably means he had some powerful enemies."

It crossed my mind that someone was trying to frame Rebecca, but I thought it rather silly to try to frame an Amish person. After all, Amish were well known for being peaceable. Amish were even excused from military duty. If someone wronged an Amish person, it was highly unlikely the Amish person would ever retaliate. No, there had to be another reason why Mr. Greaves died when he did.

I looked up as a detective strode into the room. It was Detective McCloud's partner, Carter Stirling. "Mrs. Yoder, would you come with me?" he said. "We're questioning the two of you separately."

Rebecca shot me a worried look, but I forced a smile. "It will be all right." With that, Rebecca was led away, looking over her shoulder at me.

Detective Stirling presently returned. "Please come with me, Mrs. Delight."

"Miss," I said once more. "I'm divorced."

He did not respond. I followed him through a labyrinth of rooms and corridors. These were not modernized like the lobby. The ivory tiled floor of the modern lobby gave way to dirty-colored beige floors with navy blue and chocolate brown squares dotted at random. Here the walls were all a color between a muted beige and an unpleasant yellow, and the doorframes were teal. It wasn't the nicest color combination I had ever seen.

Detective Stirling opened a wooden door and nodded inside. "We'll be right with you," he said.

The first thing I noticed about the room was that the charcoal-colored carpet looked new. Nothing else in the room was new. The old table, which appeared to be pine laminate on top, had black metal legs, as did the three chairs, which were upholstered in a faded blue fabric.

As he had said 'we', I sat at the side of the table that only had a single chair. I looked around me. The walls were pale blue, although for some reason a narrow wooden panel ran horizontally around the entire room. Directly opposite me was a huge piece of black felt, pinned onto which were several large maps. To my left was the window with vertical drapes overlooking the parking lot.

After I sat there for some time, I swiveled around. A huge whiteboard was permanently fixed to the wall behind me, but I couldn't see any cameras in the room. I wondered if they were leaving me here alone to unnerve me in the hopes I would confess.

I did my best to dispel the fanciful thoughts. Of

course the detectives weren't doing such a thing to me. The whole idea was preposterous. Besides, if they really did think I was a murderer, then surely I would be in one of those interview rooms that had a two-way mirror, just like the ones on TV.

I took comfort in that thought for a few moments, but the time stretched on. It was a great relief when the door finally opened and in stepped Detective McCloud. "Sorry to keep you waiting, Mrs. Delight," he said. He almost sounded genuine.

"Miss," I corrected him automatically.

He did not respond, but sat on the chair opposite me while Detective Stirling sat on the chair to his immediate left. They both consulted their notes for some time without speaking and I wondered once more if this could be a technique designed to put me ill at ease.

"Now, would you please go over the events of the morning?" Detective Stirling said.

"I've already been over them a hundred times," I said, and then amended that to, "At least twice."

"We need to make sure nothing has been overlooked," Detective McCloud said, and then looked at me expectantly.

I steeled myself. "I was in the cupcake store with my sister, Rebecca. Mr. Greaves came in. He told my sister he had increased his offer to sell. She said she wouldn't sell under any circumstances. He said it would be better for her if she did. I asked if he was threatening her and he said he wasn't, although he said it sarcastically, and I was sure he *was* threatening her. Then he snatched a sample chocolate cupcake and ate it. Next thing I knew, he was on the floor." I stopped talking because my mouth had run dry. I craved a glass of water.

I was worried I was going to have a panic attack. I felt dizzy and fought the urge to run out of the room.

"Do go on," Detective Stirling said.

I took another deep breath and let it out slowly. "He fell to the floor and said, 'My heart'. I thought he must be on heart medication. I looked through his pockets for a bottle of pills, but couldn't find any. While I was doing that, my sister called 911. The paramedics got there quite quickly, and that's about it."

Detective Stirling looked up from taking notes. "That's your story?"

His words rankled. "It's the truth."

"Would you like a glass of water?" Detective McCloud asked me.

I wondered if they were playing good cop, bad

cop, but did anyone ever do that outside movies? "Yes, please," I said, and then thought I should push my luck. "Is there any chance of coffee as well?"

McCloud shot me a small smile before leaving the room.

I felt uneasy being left with Detective Stirling, but he did not speak. He merely read through his notes and tapped his pen on his notepad at intervals.

It wasn't long before Detective McCloud returned. He placed a glass of water in front of me as well as a steaming polystyrene cup of coffee. I thanked him and took a sip of the coffee. It was horribly strong and bitter, but at least it was caffeine. It was hot too. I took another sip and then a large gulp of water.

The liquid comforted me somehow, so I sat a little straighter.

"Have you remembered anything since this morning? Anything else since I spoke to you earlier?"

I shook my head. "No."

"And when did you first meet Matilda Birtwistle?"

I looked at Detective McCloud. "Matilda? Today. Today was the first time I met her."

He pushed on. "And have you ever spoken with her before?"

I shook my head. "No, I've never even seen a photo of her before. There weren't any of her in the apartment. Well, there are framed photos of people on top of Mount Everest, but you can't see their faces. They could be anyone. Today was the first time I had ever seen her or spoken with her." I wondered why he was asking about Matilda and not Eleanor.

"And so, how long have you been renting the apartment from your sister?" he continued.

"About six months," I said warily.

"And are you an avid gardener, Mrs. Delight?"

I wondered if the detectives were deliberately calling me 'Mrs.' to irritate me. Maybe it was their way of throwing me off guard, to annoy me so I would let something slip. "It's Miss," I said, becoming rather irritated. "No, I'm a terrible gardener. I like looking at flowers, but I'm not very good looking after them."

"But you were looking after the Birtwistle sisters' herb garden while they were away, weren't you?"

"My sister was initially looking after their garden, but after I moved into the apartment, I said I'd take over," I said. "Why?"

The detectives did not respond.

Detective Stirling looked up at me. "Do you have a background in biology or chemistry?"

I chuckled in spite of myself. "I don't have a background in anything like that. I was brought up Amish and then I left. I eventually went to college. My major was public relations."

Stirling continued to scribble away in his notepad. "And do you know anything about the plants the Birtwistle sisters are growing?"

I gasped. "They're not illegal, are they?"

McCloud's lips twitched. "No, they are not," he said. I thought I detected a hint of amusement in his voice. I could not resist looking at his left hand and saw there was no wedding ring on his finger. Did Scottish men wear wedding rings? I had no idea. I had thought it a habit in the entire Western world, but I really didn't know. I certainly hoped he wasn't married.

Detective Stirling cleared his throat. "Miss Delight!"

I looked at him. "Sorry?"

"I asked you if Colin Greaves had ever

threatened your sister Rebecca on previous occasions."

"Only today," I said, "and when I asked him straight out if he was threatening her, he said he wasn't. It's just that his tone was quite threatening and he didn't protest in a genuine manner. It's hard to explain without you hearing the conversation, but I'm absolutely certain it was a threat."

"And was that the first occasion you believe he was threatening your sister?"

"Yes, it was. He started coming into the cupcake store about five months ago and asking Rebecca if she would sell."

"And was your sister not happy with the price?" Stirling asked me.

"It wasn't about the money. I'm sure what he offered was a fair price, but my sister didn't want to sell," I said. "And today he said he would increase his offer, but Amish don't care about monetary things." I fought to find the right words to explain. "That's not correct really, because most of them are very business minded. But what I'm saying is that they place other values above money—you know, family and things like that."

I knew I wasn't explaining very well, but I was quite tense. Surely the police couldn't suspect my sister. After all, she was Amish. I wondered if they would suspect me of murdering Colin Greaves to protect my sister.

"And so this is your twin sister, is that correct?" Stirling asked me.

"Yes, Rebecca and I are identical twins," I told him.

"So I'm sure you feel quite protective toward your sister," Stirling continued. "Were you upset about the way Colin Greaves was treating her?"

I frowned. Yes, it looked as if that's exactly what the detectives were thinking, that I had murdered Greaves to protect my sister. "I know what you're thinking," I said, "but I didn't murder him."

"And what do you think we are thinking?" Stirling asked. His tone was measured, although cold.

"You realize my sister wouldn't have murdered anyone because she's Amish. You think after Mr. Greaves threatened my sister today, I murdered him to protect her, but that doesn't make sense."

McCloud raised one eyebrow. "How so?" he said in his delightful Scottish accent.

"Well, that would mean I had a poisoned chocolate cupcake ready to give him when he came in. How would I have known when he would come in?"

"Was that the first time Colin Greaves had eaten a sample cupcake?" Stirling asked me.

My stomach sank. "No, he ate a sample cupcake every time he came in."

"And was it always a chocolate one?" Stirling asked me.

"I'm not sure, but it most likely was a chocolate one," I conceded.

I took a gulp of the coffee and washed it down with some water. My stomach rumbled. All this talk of cupcakes was making me hungry. I really needed some cake, but I knew they wouldn't get me any, of course.

By the time the detectives allowed me to leave the interview room after giving and signing my statement, I was a shaken mess. I put on a brave face when I walked over to Rebecca in the lobby. She stood up. "What did they say? What did they ask you?" She spoke breathlessly.

"I'll tell you in the car," I said, looking around the lobby. "How did the questions go with you?"

"It wasn't nearly as bad as I thought it was going to be," she said. "The detectives were quite nice, really."

I hurried out to the parking lot with Rebecca hard on my heels. As soon as I was in my car, I asked her, "Did they ask you about Eleanor and Matilda's plants?"

Rebecca nodded vigorously. "Yes, they asked me again and again about the plants, and they asked me if I was one of those Amish people who knows a lot about herbs and healing. I told them I was just a normal Amish person, and I knew more about cupcakes than I did about healing. I told them if I need healing, I always go to the widow Beiler. They asked me if I used any of the plants in my baking." She broke off and laughed. "Imagine that! I told them I don't, of course."

I nodded. "They asked me about the herb garden and asked me when I first met Matilda," I said. "If I put two and two together, it makes me think that Eleanor and Matilda are growing a deadly herb, and that it produces the very poison that killed Colin Greaves."

CHAPTER 7

*I*t seemed my suspicions were correct. We hadn't been back in my apartment for more than fifteen minutes when the doorbell rang. "Don't answer it," Matilda said. "It's just a customer wondering why the store is shut."

I shook my head and stood up. "That was the bell to the apartment not the store."

Matilda tried to wave me back down. "We're not expecting anyone and you still haven't told us everything about the police questioning you."

I shrugged and made my way down the stairs. I opened the door and was surprised to see Detective McCloud and Detective Stirling standing there.

"We would like to take another look at your

garden and take samples," Detective McCloud said without pre-emption.

"You were speaking to me only minutes ago. Why didn't you tell me then?"

McCloud raised his eyebrows. "Did you need some sort of warning, Miss Delight?" I scowled at him. "We can always get a search warrant," he added.

I waved them inside. "Come in. And it's not my garden. It's the Birtwistle sisters' garden."

"But you've been tending it for them for the past six months." His words came out as an accusation.

I continued to glare at him. "This way," I snapped. I showed the detectives to the little garden in the walled area.

"These plants aren't labeled," Detective Stirling said. He looked up at me from over a lavender plant. "How do you identify them?"

I crossed my arms over my chest. "I don't identify them. I've already told you, I don't know anything about plants. I know that one is a lavender plant." I pointed the one he had been bending over. "But that's about all I *do* know. I really don't know one plant from another. I keep telling you, Eleanor and Matilda own this garden and I merely watered the plants for them while they were away."

Matilda marched into the courtyard. "I can identify the plants for you. What would you like to know?" She shot Stirling a dark look.

"Why don't you start by pointing out some of the plants to us? Are they all herbs?"

"Yes they are. That one is asafoetida, that is rosemary, that is dill, that one that is astragalus, that is ginger, and that is turmeric."

When she stopped to draw breath, Detective Stirling spoke. "Why do you have so many herbs? Do you use them in baking?"

Matilda nodded. "Sometimes, but we mainly use them in our home-made skincare products, and we also use them for medicinal purposes. Eleanor and I lived near Dalian in China for a few years and we learned Traditional Chinese Medicine."

McCloud raised his eyebrows. "You make your own skincare products with this stuff?"

Matilda shot him a wide smile and then patted her face with both hands. "If I told you my age, you would never believe it. These herbs are responsible for this." She released her face and then pointed to it with her right hand.

I had to admit, Matilda and Eleanor had excellent skin. Sure, their faces were sagging somewhat, but neither had so much as a wrinkle or a fine line on their entire face. Maybe I should ask them to make me some facial cream. Still, I had more pressing matters on my mind like being a suspect in a murder case.

"Do you have any plants that are poisonous?" Detective Stirling asked Matilda.

"Sure." She pointed to a pretty yellow plant. "That's henbane. We use it for coughs."

"Is it poisonous?"

"Yes." She sounded quite happy. "It causes convulsions. And that is yellow jasmine. We use it as a tonic, but in large quantities it is deadly."

"You haven't mentioned wolfsbane yet," McCloud said, his eyes narrowed.

"That's it right there." Matilda pointed to a plant with pretty purple flowers. "Wolfsbane is also known as monkshood or aconitine."

As she was speaking a chill ran up my spine. McCloud's interest in wolfsbane surely meant that the victim was murdered with wolfsbane, and here we had some in our garden. Visions of defending myself in court to a jury flashed before my mind. I didn't even know a lawyer. Well, apart from my ex-husband and his friends, of course. What was I to do?

Detective McCloud was still speaking. "And

what do you specifically use wolfsbane for? Is there a specific reason you have it growing in your garden?"

Matilda seemed surprised to be asked such a question. "Of course there is! I don't grow useless plants here. Eleanor and I take wolfsbane on occasion for colds, but it's also a good disinfectant. Only a tiny amount when taken orally, you see. It's a deadly neurotoxin so it's ever so poisonous in larger amounts."

Detective Stirling had been taking photos of the wolfsbane. He stopped abruptly. "So, you are aware of its poisonous properties?"

Matilda nodded vigorously. "Of course. Isn't everybody? Everybody knows wolfsbane is poisonous. If anyone's ever read *4:50 From Paddington*, they know just how deadly wolfsbane is."

Stirling's mouth fell open. "I'm sorry, I don't know what you mean."

"It's an Agatha Christie novel, of course."

"Oh." Stirling consulted his phone before pointing to another plant. "And what is the name of that herb?"

"Foxglove."

He nodded slowly. "I thought so. And you use this as well?"

Matilda nodded.

Stirling looked exasperated. "Exactly what do you use it for?"

"Oh, I see. Eleanor and I use foxglove as an ointment for our arthritis. I have a touch of arthritis in my knee and Eleanor has it in her ankle. It was our little accident in Mongolia, you see."

Stirling's eyebrows shot skyward. "Mongolia?"

Matilda afforded him a wide smile. "Yes, it was five years ago or so. We were galloping half-tamed horses in Mongolia. I fell off and Eleanor laughed so hard that she fell off her horse too. Serves her right!"

Detective McCloud cleared his throat. "And would you consider it a poisonous plant?"

Matilda's mouth fell open. "Of course! Even a small amount can be fatal. The deadly digitalis is from foxglove. That's why we only use it in an ointment. Agatha Christie used it in several of her books." She tapped her chin. "Let me see. *Appointment with Death*, *Crooked House*, *Postern of Fate*—oh, and what was that other one?" She looked off into the distance.

I did my best to catch her attention. I didn't think it a good idea that she was so enthusiastic about her knowledge of plant poisons or so forthcoming about just how deadly some of her plants were. My efforts were in vain.

"Why are you staring at me strangely, Jane?"

"Oh, no reason," I said lamely.

Detective Stirling shot me a hard look before addressing Matilda once more. "Do you mind if I take samples of some of your plants, Mrs. Birtwistle?"

"Of course not. Help yourself. Just don't take too much, mind you. I don't want any of my plants damaged."

Detective McCloud nodded to us. "Thank you. That will be all, ladies."

It was obvious we were being dismissed, and I wondered whether I should continue to stand there. I wondered what McCloud would do if I didn't leave. Still, the detectives didn't seem to care that I hadn't left at once, and took samples of the herbs with their gloved hands.

Matilda grabbed me by the elbow and dragged me from the courtyard. As soon as we were out of earshot, she whispered, "That was so silly!"

I was perplexed. "What was?"

"I shouldn't have said those plants were poisonous."

I sighed long and hard. "You had to be honest."

"Yes, I suppose so, but I should not have been so forthright, going on and on about how poisonous they were. On the bright side, I don't grow yew trees, or hemlock, or castor oil plants. Jane, do you think they suspect you're the murderer?"

"Yes I do. It's unlikely they suspect Rebecca given the fact that she's Amish and Amish are non-violent. They're more likely to suspect me."

Matilda nodded slowly. "Yes, they think you murdered Colin Greaves to protect your sister after he threatened her."

"Well, it wasn't really much of a threat as threats go," I explained.

"You know that and I know that, but the police probably think you played down the threat. For all they know Greaves might have threatened Rebecca on numerous occasions, and she wouldn't defend herself as she is Amish as you rightly pointed out, so they figure you've taken matters into your own hands."

I rubbed my temples hard with both hands. The tightening across the front of my head and across the bridge of my nose signaled an oncoming headache. My stomach churned and I wanted nothing more than to lie down with a cold pack on my forehead. "I hadn't thought of it like that. I'm sure that's how they'll make their case."

Matilda patted my arm in a reassuring manner. "I wouldn't worry about it. By the way, do you happen to know a good lawyer?"

I sighed. "No, I don't." *Only my ex-husband and I'm hardly likely to ask him*, I added silently.

"Then there's nothing else for it!" Matilda exclaimed. Her tone was gleeful. "We're going to have to solve the murder ourselves. The police never get it right. If the police got it right, then Miss Marple wouldn't have had anything to do. This will be my first case."

She smiled widely as she said it. "Don't you worry, Jane. We will have some coffee or meadow tea and we will make a list of suspects. Surely there must be plenty of suspects. Greaves was a very wealthy man, so he would have left an inheritance. The motives for murder are usually love, money, or wrong place-wrong time. Also, you said he didn't really threaten Rebecca, but he might have threatened other people. Plus, a man like that would have made business enemies. And then there's his wife. Perhaps she wanted to do away with him."

"What makes you say that?" I asked her. "You mean for the inheritance?"

Matilda shook her head. "Perhaps he was mean to her and finally pushed her over the edge. Maybe it was for the inheritance. Or maybe he was having an affair."

I scratched my head. "You think he was having an affair?"

She shrugged one shoulder. "I have no idea, but it's certainly a possibility we should investigate. If Greaves was having an affair, then not only would his wife want to murder him, but maybe his mistress was married and so her husband would want to murder him too. Maybe. And as Greaves obviously was still with his wife and not with his mistress, then maybe his mistress wanted to murder him as well. That gives us three suspects."

I shot her a small smile, but I thought it all rather a stretch. One thing was certain; the detectives did suspect me. I had no idea who the other suspects were and how far the police would go in their pursuit of them. As I showed the detectives out, thoughts of me giving evidence in a courtroom flashed through my mind.

CHAPTER 8

*R*ebecca, Matilda, and I hurried back up the stairs to the apartment. Matilda was brimming with enthusiasm about working on her first case. When I walked into the living room, I nearly fell over the cat. "Mr. Crumbles, what are you doing?" I said in alarm.

Eleanor hurried over. "What is he playing with?"

"It's a set of keys," I said. "They're not mine. Are they yours?" I looked from Eleanor to Matilda and back again.

Both shook their heads. The cat gave the keys a huge shove with his paw and they shot across the room. In a few seconds the cat was on top of them, sending them in the other direction. "I'll have to get him his own set of keys," Eleanor said with a smile.

"You're missing the point, Eleanor," Matilda said in a scolding tone. "Someone owns those keys and your cat has stolen them."

Eleanor gasped. "How could you say such a thing about my cat? And have you completely lost your mind, Matilda? Cats can't steal keys."

The bell to the apartment rang once and then rang again a few times in quick succession. "I'll get it," I said. I opened the door to see Detective McCloud. "Haven't you left already?" I said. I realized my tone was snappy. It came out more curt than I intended it.

"I've misplaced my keys," he said, scratching his head in bewilderment. "You mind if I have a look around the herb garden?"

"Oh, I think the cat might have your keys. Come with me."

Mr. Crumbles was still playing with the keys, pushing them with his paw and pouncing on them with great delight. "Are those your keys?" I asked the detective.

He chuckled and bent over the cat. He carefully reached out his hand and stroked Mr. Crumbles and then took the keys. "How did he get them?"

"Well, I didn't give them to him," I said. I felt quite defensive. After all, I was no doubt the prime suspect in a murder case.

The detective did not respond. After tickling Mr. Crumbles under his chin, he straightened up. "Thank you, ladies. That's one mystery solved."

I nodded to Matilda as a silent signal to show the detective out. She didn't take the hint. I ducked my head slightly in his direction, but she simply stared at me. "What is it, Jane?" she finally asked. "Is your neck sore?"

I gave up. "I'll show you out, Detective," I said in a resigned fashion.

When we were at the door, I opened the front door for him. "I didn't take your keys," I said. "I know it sounds strange, but the cat did it."

To my surprise, he chuckled. "I believe you," he said. I nodded and shut the door and then leaned back against it.

I knew I was innocent, but I was sure that prisons were filled with innocent people. Or maybe not filled, but there had to be some innocent people incarcerated and I did not want to become one of them. I hurried up the stairs. "I forgot to ask Detective McCloud when you can open the store again."

"They already told me. I can open it now, but I'm not going to. Matilda was just telling me that you're the prime suspect. I think we should all put our heads together to try to figure out who it could be."

I was touched. "Are you sure?"

Rebecca nodded. "I'll make us all some meadow tea."

Eleanor jumped to her feet. "You stay right there. I'll make the tea and some nice coffee as well."

I hid a smile. I suspected my sister always gave Eleanor and Matilda meadow tea, but they far preferred strong coffee.

Soon we were sitting around sipping a hot beverage, and a large plate containing delightful whoopie pies and slices of Shoo-fly pie was sitting in front of us.

Matilda's pen hovered over a large sheet of paper. "Now let's write down the suspects," she said. "The only two we know for certain are Rebecca and Jane."

Rebecca and I winced. Matilda pushed on. "Let's make a list of the other suspects. His wife, his mistress…"

Rebecca interrupted her. "Colin Greaves had a mistress?"

Matilda shrugged. "Who knows? But I'm going to write down 'mistress' because we don't want to leave anyone out. I am also writing, 'His mistress's husband'." She nodded to Rebecca. "We don't know if he had a mistress or if his alleged mistress had a husband, but we need to write that down. Oh, and then any heirs. Also, people he threatened. I have written 'Heirs' and underlined it and I've written 'People he threatened' and underlined it. There are also people he had business dealings with. I'll make that another heading." She underlined the last with such a flourish, her pen flew off the page. Mr. Crumbles looked up at her, no doubt hoping the pen would fly away and he could play with it.

"And of course, William and Mia Willow, the owners of the health food and supplements store, who also refused to sell to Colin Greaves. Maybe Greaves threatened them a little harder and they retaliated. Eleanor, fetch my laptop, will you?"

Eleanor trotted out of the room and presently returned with a laptop. She handed it to Matilda.

"No, you search on it and I'll do the writing,"

Matilda said. "Have you ever seen Miss Marple do her own searching on a computer? Indeed not! She leaves that for others."

"They didn't have computers in Miss Marple's time," Eleanor pointed out.

Matilda made a tut-tutting sound with her tongue. "Always the critic, Eleanor. Always the critic. Now see what you can find out about Colin Greaves. Find out the name of his wife and find out the names of his children. That's the first thing you are to do."

I expected Eleanor to take a while, but she proved to be a deft hand at computers. "His wife's name is Stephanie," she announced. "They have only one son, Brooks. There's a photo of him here and he looks like a criminal."

"Move that laptop around here so we can all see," Matilda ordered her.

I peered at the screen. "He doesn't look like a criminal to me. He looks like someone who spends all his time in the gym."

Eleanor nodded sagely. "Exactly! That's how it starts."

I was quite confused. "How what starts?" I shot Rebecca a look. She was sipping her tea. No doubt she was used to the sisters.

"Yes, it all starts at the gym. They get hooked on steroids and then the steroid dealer of course deals in other drugs. So then they become drug addicts and then they turn to crime to fund their drug habit."

Matilda snorted rudely. "Are you saying Brooks murdered his father to get the inheritance so he could spend it on drugs?"

Eleanor shot her a dark look. "You have a better idea?"

Unperturbed, Matilda pushed on. "Now, Eleanor, see if he has a mistress, and see if you can find out anything about the mistress."

Eleanor threw both hands into the air. "Mistresses are secret, Matilda. If he had a mistress, it certainly wouldn't be on the computer."

"Well then, see if there's any scandal about him, and while you're at it, look for business dealings."

My spirits fell. *This is not looking good for me*, I thought. Aloud, I said, "We have two definite suspects, his wife, Stephanie, and his son, Brooks. No doubt he was worth millions, and we should find out exactly who is the beneficiary of his will."

"Perhaps Stephanie and Brooks were in it together," Matilda said. "In Agatha Christie books, often two or more people are in it together."

Rebecca suddenly spoke up. "We need to do a lot of baking this afternoon, Jane. The police took all the cupcakes, so we have to replenish them before tomorrow."

I drew my thoughts from the murder investigation to the more pressing matter of the store. "Yes, you're right."

"We can think and pray as we work," Rebecca said. "That will clear our minds and maybe something will occur to us."

"I've got it!" Eleanor suddenly shrieked, causing the rest of us to jump. Even Mr. Crumbles ran under a sideboard. "It says here that Colin Greaves cheated some people. He had an investment scheme developing property that didn't exist. It says here that people lost millions."

"Does it mention them by name?" Matilda said, leaning over so she could see the screen.

"No, it doesn't mention any individual names," Eleanor said, "so I'll have to search and find out their names. It says Greaves cheated individuals into investing in projects that did not materialize."

"Good work, Eleanor," Matilda said, although she said it in a begrudging manner.

Rebecca agreed. "Before the store opens

tomorrow, Jane and I should visit with Wanda Hershberger. Her daughter works in the medical examiner's office. We should be able to find out the poison that was used on Mr. Greaves."

"How would she know that information?" I asked Rebecca.

"Her daughter does filing at the medical examiner's office. I'm sure she would know. Wanda can ask her to find out. In fact, I'll call her from the store phone now and ask her to find out and tell us tomorrow."

"But Wanda Hershberger is an Amish name," I said. "Is she Amish? How will you call her?"

"Wanda lives in a *grossmammi haus* behind her daughter's house, and her daughter's husband has a carpentry business in the barn near the house. He has a phone there so I'll call and leave a message."

"Good idea," I said. To Eleanor and Matilda, I said, "A *grossmammi haus* means 'grandmother house'. It's a little house behind a main house, where grandmothers might live."

Matilda set down her pen and paper. "Yes, I know that, Jane. Rebecca, I'm surprised you're getting involved in this. It's not quite an Amish thing to do, is it?"

Rebecca chuckled. "Mer sott em sei Eegne net verlosse; Gott verlosst die Seine niche."

Matilda looked at me, her eyes raised. "I don't know that one!"

I translated. "One should not abandon one's own; God does not abandon His own."

CHAPTER 9

The following morning I collected Rebecca from her house and she directed me to Wanda Hershberger's house. It was early in the morning, but not early for an Amish person, as I well knew from my childhood. I stifled a yawn. Rebecca and I had been up late baking.

When we arrived, I followed Rebecca around behind the main house to a small *grossmammi haus* in the yard. Small and white with a red roof, it looked like a miniature version of the main house. I didn't see Wanda's daughter, so I figured she was already on her way to work, and by the sounds coming out of the barn, it seemed Wanda's son-in-law was already at work in his carpentry business.

"*Hiya* Rebecca," Mrs. Hershberger greeted my sister. "*Guten mariye*."

"Good morning, Wanda. Do you remember my sister, Jane?"

Mrs. Hershberger smiled at me. "Of course, but I wouldn't recognize you now. You're so much older. A great deal older, in fact. Oh well, age comes to us all."

Thanks a lot, I thought. Aloud I said, "It's nice to see you again, Mrs. Hershberger."

"Please call me Wanda. I'm about to have breakfast. Please come in. I was about to have scrapple and *kaffi* soup."

I hadn't eaten either coffee soup or scrapple in years. I was trying to watch my weight, and I thought about refusing the scrapple as we sat down to the old oak table in the little kitchen. Still, the delightful scent of deep-fried scrapple, the pork scraps and trimmings with flour, cornmeal, and spices, cut into slices and pan-fried until crispy brown, was simply irresistible.

"Would you like it with apple butter, jelly, maple syrup, or ketchup?" Wanda asked us.

I asked for apple butter while Rebecca selected maple syrup. The scrapple was served with eggs and fried potatoes. I had all but forgotten the hearty Amish breakfast of my youth. These days, I simply had coffee for breakfast. Presently, Wanda asked, "Would you like cereal topped with fruit or would you prefer *kaffi* soup?"

I toyed with asking for coffee soup since I hadn't had time for coffee that morning and I was already feeling somewhat caffeine-deprived, but I had never liked coffee soup before and I didn't think I would like it now. Coffee soup consisted of bits of bread broken up and placed in a bowl with coffee and warm milk poured over the top. "I'd like some cereal with fruit, please," I said, and Rebecca had the same.

To my relief, Wanda filled a large mug of coffee and passed it to me. I took a sip and sighed with delight. There was something different, something comforting, about Amish coffee. It reminded me of my youth, the happy family life, the close-knit community with everyone doing their best to help others out. Still, I was used to my non-Amish—or as the Amish called it, English—ways by now and I would never be able to return to the Amish way of life. That still didn't rule out the waves of nostalgia that overwhelmed me from time to time.

I was anxious to find out the news from the medical examiner's office, but I knew it couldn't be rushed. I waited for Rebecca to ask Wanda.

It turned out that she didn't have to. "So, Rebecca, the *Englischer* who died in your store. You want to know what made him die?"

I leaned across the table. Rebecca said, "*Jah, denki*."

"It was poison."

My spirits sank. I don't know what I had been expecting. What else could it have been?

Rebecca nodded. I wondered how she could be so calm, and I knew it was her unwavering faith in God's will. "Yes, I figured it was poison as the detectives took herb plants from our garden, so we were certain it was one of those. Did your daughter find out exactly what the poison was?"

"Yes, she did. It was wolfsbane."

"Aha!" I said. "One of the detectives did mention wolfsbane more than the other herbs."

Wanda narrowed her eyes. "And you have wolfsbane growing in your garden?"

"Yes we do," Rebecca said, "and I believe the police see us as suspects."

"That would make sense," Wanda said after she

took a large gulp of coffee. "After all, the *mann* did die in your store and you are growing the very poison that killed him."

"But surely the police would think it quite silly of us to poison someone with a poisonous plant that we were growing," I said.

Wanda shook her head. "My daughter always says that criminals aren't that clever. That's why they get caught."

My spirits sank even further. This was not good, not good at all. What was I to do? More and more I was looking like the prime suspect. Something occurred to me. "Did your daughter happen to mention if he was poisoned long before he died?"

Wanda furrowed her brow. "What do you mean?"

"Well, he ate a cupcake in Rebecca's store and collapsed soon after. What if someone had poisoned him at his home say five hours earlier and the poison took five hours to work?" I was so anxious that I wasn't choosing my words well.

"I wonder if someone was trying to frame us?" Rebecca said. "He was poisoned with wolfsbane and we have wolfsbane growing in the garden. That seems a little too much of a coincidence."

"Yes, I'm sure that's what the police think," Wanda said, a remark that did not help my anxiety at all.

My stomach knotted and I fought rising panic.

"There's no point worrying about it," Wanda said. "You just have to find out when the man was actually poisoned. Maybe it was as you said, that he was poisoned some time ago. Or maybe it was in the cupcake, which means someone had to have placed that cupcake there. Rebecca, who knows the Birtwistle sisters grow poisonous plants or wolfsbane on your property?"

Rebecca bit her lip. "I don't know. Eleanor and Matilda had been on a cruise for months, so they couldn't have told anyone recently. I certainly haven't told anyone. Have you, Jane?"

I shook my head. "No, I haven't. I've been watering the plants, but I'm sure I haven't told anyone. Besides, I don't really know anyone. Not any more."

"So your daughter found out it was definitely wolfsbane, but she didn't mention when the poison was actually administered?" Rebecca asked Wanda.

"That's exactly right," she said. "Why don't you go and ask Sarah Beiler?"

I looked at Rebecca. "Sarah Beiler is the local

healer," she said. "Most people from the community go to her if they have ailments. She knows a lot about herbs for medicinal purposes. May be she can tell us about wolfsbane. She will know the amount needed to poison someone and whether the taste could be disguised in a chocolate cupcake."

Something occurred to me. "Wanda, would you mind finding out from your daughter whether or not the medical examiner could tell whether the poison was in the cupcake itself?"

"Sure, I'll ask her," Wanda said.

"And the police took all the cupcakes from my store," Rebecca added. "I don't suppose the medical examiner's office checks the contents of those?"

Wanda looked confused. "What do you mean?" Before either of us could respond, she said, "Ah, I see what you mean. *Nee*, I have no idea if that's the medical examiner's department. It might be a different department." She chuckled. "All my daughter talks about is her work filing in the medical examiner's office, but I haven't learned much about it."

I forced a smile. This was not looking good, not good at all. I'm sure the murderer had no way of knowing we were growing wolfsbane in the garden.

If he or she did, then it would seem Rebecca and I were being framed. After all, Colin Greaves did die in Rebecca's store. I made a mental note to find out how long wolfsbane would take to prove fatal after it was administered. Sarah Beiler would be the one to answer that question.

CHAPTER 10

When we got back to the cupcake store, it was almost time to open. Rebecca and I hurried around getting everything ready. "Should we visit with Sarah Beiler this afternoon?" I asked her.

Rebecca set out several small cupcakes on a plate. "I'll never be able to look at the sample cupcakes in the same way again. Sorry, what did you say? Oh yes, Sarah Beiler. No, I think it's fairly urgent. Why don't you go now? You could take Matilda and Eleanor with you."

"Are you sure you'll be all right in the shop alone? Do you think Eleanor or Matilda should stay with you?"

An unmistakable look of fear flashed across

Rebecca's face. She held both hands in front of her, palms outward. "*Nee, nee, nee*! I don't need their help. I'll be fine by myself. You can take both of them with you."

I suspected there had been an incident with either Matilda or Eleanor at some point, but I wasn't about to ask. I had more pressing things on my mind like being a suspect in a murder case. "All right, I'll go. Do you think she'll be upset to have three *Englischers* arrive at her door?"

Rebecca laughed. "She has several *Englischers* as customers. I'm sure you won't frighten her. Speak to her in Pennsylvania Dutch to put her at ease."

I laughed too.

"Did I hear my name mentioned?" Matilda said, hurrying into the shop.

I told her what we had discussed and concluded, "So, would you and Eleanor like to come with me?"

Matilda's face lit up. "Sure! I'll run and tell Eleanor to get ready."

In less than five minutes, both ladies appeared once more in the shop. There hadn't been any customers in that time, so I hoped it would be a slow morning. "Rebecca, call me if you get too many customers and I'll drive straight back." I waved my cell phone at her.

"I'm sure it will be fine."

I looked at Eleanor. Her hair was still full of rollers. "How long will it take you to get ready?"

Eleanor looked puzzled. "I'm ready now."

"I see." I had not known Eleanor long, but I had not once seen her without her rollers. It made me wonder if she ever took them out. If so, why were they in? I figured she was going to take them out to look good for an occasion. But what occasion could that be? Still, I was beginning to realize that the Birtwistle sisters were somewhat unusual. They had certainly brightened up my life in a short space of time.

"All right then, let's go."

"Where are we going again?" Eleanor asked me.

Matilda waved a finger at her. "Honestly, Eleanor. Sometimes I wonder about you. I told you quite clearly that we are going to see an herbalist. Is that what she is, Jane, an herbalist?"

"She's Amish and she's a healer," I told them. "She uses herbs and has a good knowledge of them, so we can ask questions about wolfsbane."

"Do you think we will frighten her?" Eleanor asked me.

"Quite possibly," Matilda said, looking Eleanor up and down. "What are we are waiting for? Come on, there's no time like the present."

On the ride over to Sarah Beiler's house, Matilda and Eleanor kept me entertained with stories of their world travels. It was good having the company. I had been worried about how I would handle being with other people. I had been alone for six months—more than that really, as I was pretty much alone when married as my husband was never home, but I thoroughly enjoyed the company of these ladies. What's more, they made me laugh.

"Take the next left," Matilda suddenly yelled.

"But that's not the way," I said, puzzled.

"Left!" Matilda exclaimed. "You told us you thought you were being followed, and I'm sure that car has been behind us the whole way."

I took the next left as she asked, but the car didn't follow us. "It wasn't someone following me after all," I said.

"Or maybe it's someone who is experienced at tailing," Matilda said. "That's exactly what I would do if I were tailing someone. Head for Mrs. Beiler's house now and I'll keep a good eye out."

The rest of the journey passed without incident. I parked the car and got out and then walked over to the horse tied to the rail outside the house. He was a beautiful bay horse. I stroked his glossy neck. "The one thing I miss about the Amish way of life, apart from the community being so tight knit and helping everybody, is the horses," I told Matilda and Eleanor. "I really miss horses."

"Then why don't you buy one?" Eleanor said.

Matilda looked at Eleanor over the top of her glasses. "Yes, I'm sure Rebecca would be thrilled when Jane takes a horse into her cupcake store, or maybe she can take the horse up the stairs into our apartment."

Eleanor was not one to bite back, being a kindly person. "Obviously I didn't mean she would keep the horse in our apartment, of course, Matilda," she said in even tones. "She could keep the horse somewhere and pay board. Isn't there a name for that?" Without waiting for any one to respond, she pushed on. "Of course, why didn't I think of that? She could keep the horse at Rebecca's farm."

"As much as I love horses, they're expensive," I said. "If I get a horse, I'll get a rescue horse. In fact,

I would get an old rescue horse because most people don't rescue elderly animals."

"It's lucky we're not rescue animals, then," Matilda said with a chuckle.

"Tell me about it!" I said. I spotted someone peeping behind the curtains so I made my way to the door. As my hand was raised to knock, an Amish woman opened the door.

"*Guten mariye*," I said, greeting her. "I'm Rebecca Yoder's twin sister, Jane. These ladies are sisters, Matilda and Eleanor Birtwistle, and they live in the apartment above Rebecca's cupcake store."

Sarah at first looked confused, but then she smiled widely. "I'm Sarah Beiler," she said, "but I think you already know that. Won't you come in?"

She ushered us into her house. Once more, I was struck by just how quiet Amish houses are. There was no low vibration of electricity, no electric refrigerator humming away, no low sound of the television, or any of the sounds that people never notice until they're suddenly bereft of them. Amish houses were always quiet unless it was the cheerful sound of children's laughter or happy conversation.

Once we were seated in comfortable wooden chairs, Sarah abruptly left the room. She presently returned carrying a tray on which were steaming mugs. I noticed a big plate of whoopie pies of every color imaginable. She set them in front of us and we thanked her.

I took a sip of the tea. Peppermint. I was quite partial to meadow tea.

"Now what can I do for you ladies?" Sarah asked.

"Yesterday, a man died in my sister's store."

I expected Sarah to gasp or at least look shocked, but she nodded slowly.

"Did you already know?" I asked her.

"*Jah*," she said, nodding. "My brother Michael told me. Rebecca told her husband, of course, and her husband works with Elijah, a friend of my brother Michael."

"Oh." That made sense. News usually traveled like wildfire around the Amish community. "We have just found out that the victim, Colin Greaves, was killed with wolfsbane."

That was news to Sarah. She raised her eyebrows and then said, "I see."

Matilda spoke for the first time. "We grow wolfsbane in our greenhouse along with several other herbs that are poisonous in certain quantities."

"You use the herbs medicinally?" Sarah asked.

Eleanor and Matilda nodded.

Sarah looked pleased. "Maybe we could talk at some time."

"I'd like that," Eleanor said, and Matilda nodded.

"So you've come to ask me about the wolfsbane, how it specifically relates to the victim?" Sarah asked.

I noticed her eyes were like a hawk's. Nothing would escape this lady. She was as sharp as a tack.

"Rebecca and I were there when Mr. Greaves entered the shop," I told her. "He was talking for some time, maybe about five minutes, and then he ate one of the sample cupcakes. Rebecca always has them on the countertop. He ate a chocolate one. Shortly after doing so, he clutched his throat and fell to the ground. Rebecca called 911 and then the paramedics took him away. The detectives came soon after and then one of them got a call that Mr. Greaves had passed away."

Sarah had been listening intently, leaning forward, her vivid green eyes fixed on me. "Did he say anything?" she asked me.

I tapped my head. "Oh yes he did! I almost forgot. He said, 'My heart'. I thought it must have been because he had a heart condition and needed his heart medication. I looked through his coat pockets, but there were no bottles of medication."

Sarah shook her head. "He would have been saying that because he was suffering ventricular tachycardia. You know, abnormal, rapid heart rate. That's one of the main symptoms of wolfsbane. "

She looked around the three of us. "Are any of you familiar with what wolfsbane does, as a poison, I mean?"

We all shook our heads.

"If eaten, it causes neurological and gastrointestinal symptoms as well as cardiovascular symptoms, and the ventricular tachycardias are often fatal."

"So what we were hoping you could tell us," I began, "is this. Obviously, Mr. Greaves was given a fatal dose of wolfsbane. How long would it take a fatal dose to cause symptoms? I guess I'm asking whether the wolfsbane was definitely in that chocolate cupcake in Rebecca's store or whether he could have been given it before he entered the store."

"That's a hard one," Sarah said. "It could have been given fifteen minutes before, maybe much longer. How long after he ate the cupcake did symptoms show?"

"Immediately, really," I said. I tried to remember. It was only the previous day, after all. I figured I'd be a terrible witness in a court case because I was having trouble remembering little details of only the previous day.

"I think that's too soon," Sarah said. "I can't be sure, mind you. Maybe there was a huge dose in the cupcake, but I would say he was given it before he entered the store. Would you say he was in there about five minutes before the symptoms showed?"

I nodded.

Sarah looked thoughtful, and then said, "In my opinion he was given it before he entered the store. Did the police take samples of the cupcakes?"

"They took them all," I told her. "And what's more, we had several customers that day who ate the sample cupcakes. One of them was a regular customer and she's okay. The police contacted her and she doesn't have a single symptom. The police actually took every cupcake in the store, and if they found poison in any of them, they haven't told us. We were up late last night baking to replace them all."

"I'd be very surprised if the poison was in the cupcake in that case," Sarah said. "I'd say it was administered before he entered the store."

"And you think it would take at least fifteen minutes before he had symptoms?" I asked her.

"Yes, about fifteen minutes," she said.

"I know people can build up an immunity to poison if taken in small amounts over time," Matilda said, "but I also know that thallium is fatal if given over time in small doses. Is there any possibility he could have been given wolfsbane in small doses and this was the straw that broke the camel's back, so to speak?"

Sarah shook her head. "No, that's unlikely. It seems somebody administered him a fatal dose before he entered the store. As I said, it would be a minimum of fifteen minutes before symptoms appeared."

"Is it dose-dependent?" I asked her. "What if he was given a huge dose in the cupcake? Would that have caused instant death?"

Once more, Sarah shook her head. "*Nee*, it would still take about fifteen minutes."

"*Denki*. You've been ever so helpful," I said.

"Yes, thank you so much for your time," Matilda said. "How much do we owe you for this consultation?"

"Nothing at all," Sarah said. "My advice is free, but perhaps you could do me one favor?"

"Sure," Eleanor said. "What is it?"

"You know how we had the heavy rain last night?" We all nodded. Sarah pushed on. "My roof is leaking and I'm wondering if there's something wrong with it. Would one of you ladies climb up onto the roof to take a look?"

"Sure," Matilda said.

"I'll go up on the roof," I said.

"Let Jane go," Eleanor said. "She's the youngest one here."

"That makes a pleasant change," I said with a laugh. "Do you have a ladder?"

"Yes, I'll fetch it for you," Sarah said.

Thankfully, the ladder was metal and not an old wooden one that was likely to give way. "Matilda and I will hold it steady for you, Jane," Eleanor said. I thanked them and shimmied up the ladder, thankful I was not wearing a skirt.

The roof wasn't steep, but it was slippery and I was afraid I'd fall off. I was a little concerned. Sarah walked about the front, guiding me and pointing this way and that. "Over to the right. No too far! Go back a bit toward the road. Yes, right about there!"

I bent down and peered at the roof. I could see the problem. "There doesn't appear to be a hole in your roof, but your gutters are full of leaves," I yelled down to Sarah. "You'll need to get all the gutters around your house cleaned out soon."

"Thank you, Jane," Sarah called out. "I'm relieved it's only a matter of leaves in the gutters. "

"They're packed full of leaves," I said.

"Would you mind just checking over the back of the roof and seeing if the gutters are full over that side as well?"

My heart sank. All I wanted to do was to get off the roof as quickly as possible, but I wanted to help Sarah. "Okay," I said in a small voice. I carefully lowered myself over the roof. I wasn't one for heights.

Eleanor's voice rang out. "Quick, you've gotta come down now, Jane! Hurry!"

I wondered what the urgency was. I had heard a car so I figured Sarah had another customer and it was time for us to go.

"I'm coming!" I called out. I lowered myself over the ridge of the roof and took one step. My foot gave way and I slid down the roof wildly scratching for something to grab. There was nothing.

I screamed as I flew over the edge of the roof, my eyes tightly shut. I felt like it was all happening in slow motion. I had thoughts of landing with broken limbs.

To my surprise, a pair of strong arms wrapped around me and then I had a soft landing. I opened my eyes. Sarah, Matilda, and Eleanor were bending over me. Eleanor and Sarah's faces were white and drawn, but Matilda was doing her best not to laugh. A grunting noise came from under me and the ground shook. I looked down and to my utter embarrassment realized I had landed right on top of Detective McCloud.

"Are you hurt?" he said in a pained voice.

I held out my hands so the ladies could help me to my feet. I clung onto Eleanor as a wave of nausea hit me. After a moment, I managed to say, "I'm all right. Are you?"

He clutched his ribs and lay on the ground a bit longer. "Just winded," he said, patting his ribs. "I don't think anything is broken." Suddenly, he scrambled to his feet, one hand on his ribs.

"Thank you for saving me," I said.

He shot me a warm smile, but then his official mask was over his face once more. "Do you ladies know Mrs. Beiler well?"

Here we go again, I thought. *He's suspicious.* "We just met her today," I said. "Since I'm obviously a suspect in the murder case, we've come to ask her about the wolfsbane. We wanted to know how long the symptoms would take to show after the victim was poisoned."

"And she said a minimum of fifteen minutes," Matilda offered.

Detective McCloud raised his eyebrows. "What makes you say that?" he asked Sarah.

"Well, I would think that's common knowledge about wolfsbane," she said.

He folded his arms over his chest. "Wolfsbane? Who said the poison was wolfsbane?"

"The whole Amish community knows," I said, and then sent up a silent prayer for forgiveness for not being completely honest. At any rate, I was sure the whole Amish community *would* know within the next few hours.

He nodded slowly. "I see."

"And as the victim died in my presence, and as there is wolfsbane growing on the premises, I figure I'm a suspect so…" I would have said more but Matilda interrupted me.

"So we decided to do some investigating of our own," Matilda said, ignoring my warning look.

Detective McCloud drew himself up to his full

height. "Investigating! Please ladies, don't do anything of the sort."

"That's what they always say to Miss Marple," Matilda said.

I bit back a smile. I could see Detective McCloud had no idea how to respond to Matilda.

"That might be so, but this is real life not fiction," he said sternly, "and I don't want you ladies in danger. I'm asking you not to do any investigating and to keep right out of it."

Matilda shot him a wide smile. "Whatever you say, Officer." She continued to smile widely. Matilda wouldn't win an Oscar, and no doubt it was as clear to Detective McCloud as it was to me that she had every intention of investigating the case.

"And when did you first meet these ladies?" he asked Sarah.

"Today, as they said," she said.

"Thank you." He gave her a small bow.

Sarah shot me a questioning look. "He's Scottish," I said. "They don't have Amish people in Scotland so I think he doesn't know how to act around you."

Before Sarah could respond, Detective McCloud said, "May I speak with you in private, Mrs. Beiler?"

"We were just leaving anyway," I said. "Thanks so much for your help, Sarah."

"And thank you for checking my roof," she said. "I'm sorry you fell off. You could have been badly hurt."

The detective turned to me. "Yes, you could have been hurt," he said. "Please don't do anything so reckless again. If I hadn't been here to catch you, goodness knows what would have happened to you."

I did not know how to react. I mean, it was nice of him to be concerned, but then again, I was a grown woman and I wasn't breaking the law.

I drove back to Rebecca's store with conflicting emotions and the memory of the detective's strong arms wrapped around me.

CHAPTER 11

hen I got back to the cupcake store, there were several customers milling around. I hurried behind the counter to help. "Why didn't you call me?" I whispered to Rebecca.

"They all came in at once," she said. "I was just about to call you. How did it go?"

"Sarah said the poison wouldn't have been in the cupcake," I told her. "She said it would have been administered at least fifteen minutes before he collapsed."

Rebecca simply nodded and served a customer. We were rushed for the next five minutes and then the shop cleared. "What are we going to do now?" I asked Rebecca.

"I don't know," she said. "I must say, I'm so relieved the poison wasn't in the cupcake. Surely the police must know that, though?"

Before I could respond, Matilda walked through the front door. "I'm here as a customer," she said. "I'd like to buy some apple pie cupcakes."

Rebecca waved one hand at her. "Nonsense, Matilda. You know you can always have the schnitz pie cupcakes for free, or any cupcakes for that matter."

"I insist," Matilda said. "Anyway, I think I want to go and ask those health supplement store owners questions."

Rebecca frowned. "William and Mia Willow?"

"Yes, that's them. I don't really know them, but I've bought a few things from that store. When will Jane have time to come with me?"

"After we close," I said, but then I tapped myself on the side of my head. "How silly of me. They no doubt close when we do."

Rebecca wiped the countertop. "Why not wait for another five minutes and if no more customers come, you go and speak with them then. They're only around the corner."

"Maybe I could ask Eleanor to help you in here," Matilda said to Rebecca.

Rebecca's face went white. "No. Not after the last incident."

Finally, my curiosity got the better of me. "What happened?"

"Never you mind," Matilda said as she disappeared out the door.

"She forgot the cupcakes," Rebecca said.

"I'm sure she'll be back for them," I said with a chuckle. "Rebecca, what can you tell me about William and Mia Willow? I mean, I've bought stuff in their store, but I don't really know them as such."

"They seem nice," Rebecca said. "I don't know why they refused to sell to Mr. Greaves. What will you say to them?"

"I'm just going to be forthright. I'm going to come straight out and ask them why they didn't sell to him, and ask them if they are suspects in the murder too."

Rebecca gasped. "You can't!"

"Why not? What's the worst that can happen?"

Rebecca's jaw continued to hang open. Finally, she said, "Why don't you go now? No one's been here and you won't be away long."

I hurried up the stairs to the apartment. Matilda was watching an episode of *Miss Marple*. "I'm watching *4:50 from Paddington*," she said gleefully. "It was also released as *What Mrs. McGillicuddy Saw*. A vic was poisoned with monkshood in that too. Oh, in case you've forgotten, monkshood is wolfsbane."

"Who was the murderer in that one?" I asked her.

Matilda winked at me. "Now that would be telling."

"Who was murdered?"

"Lots of people," Matilda said happily.

I decided to change the subject. "Are you both coming with me too, Eleanor, or is it just you, Matilda?"

"I have to wash my hair," Eleanor said, adjusting one of the rollers in her hair.

I nodded. I wondered if the rollers would still be in her hair when I returned. "Now, where are my keys? I left them there on the coffee table."

"You will need to put them up high on a hook," Eleanor said. "Mr. Crumbles likes to take them, if you recall."

How could I have forgotten? I walked out of the room to look for the cat and saw him just outside the laundry room. Sure enough, he was alternating between standing on his hind legs and pouncing on the keys. I hurried over to him, but just as I did, he swiped at the keys with his left paw. They flew through the air into the laundry room. I hurried in there and let out a shriek.

Matilda abandoned Miss Marple and hurried over. "What's happened? The way you yelled, I thought there was an intruder."

"Mr. Crumbles hit the keys directly into his litter tray," I said with a sigh.

"I changed it only this morning," Eleanor said. "It could be worse. Much worse."

I reached in, fetched the keys, and then washed them. Luckily, my keys were not electronic as I could only afford an old car after my husband had run off with Cherri. I pulled a face as the memories hit me all at once.

Matilda touched my arm. "Come on, we have some sleuthing to do."

"I don't know what's wrong with me today!" I exclaimed. "I don't need the keys. The health food store is only a short walk away."

Both Eleanor and Matilda laughed and I joined in their laughter.

"Too much on your mind, dear," Matilda said.

As Matilda and I walked to the store, she asked me what my plan was.

"Plan?" I asked, aghast. "Am I supposed to have a plan?" Before she could answer, I added, "I don't have a plan as such. I'm simply going to tell them the truth."

"You're going to ask them if they murdered the vic?"

I grimaced. "Not exactly, but I'm going to tell them that he died in Rebecca's store. I'll tell them that it was wolfsbane. Actually, no—I'll tell them it was a poisonous herb."

"You won't tell them it was wolfsbane?" she asked me.

I shook my head. "No, because I should leave that to the police, but everybody probably knows by now that Colin Greaves was poisoned. It won't hurt to say that. Anyway, I'm going to play it by ear."

The interior of the health food store was freshly painted a most unpleasant shade of green. No doubt the owners liked it or they wouldn't have painted it that color. Matilda must have been thinking the same thing, as she whispered to me, "Everyone has different tastes. Each to their own."

I readily agreed. It was difficult to maneuver in the store as it was crammed full of organic food, organic shampoo, all sorts of vitamin supplements and protein powders. "Do you buy much stuff in here?" I asked Matilda.

"Not really," she said. "We mostly grow our

own, but on occasion I do buy something from here. If you're wondering if I know the owners well enough to question them, then no. I'm going to leave that to you."

"Great," I muttered. I took a deep breath and prepared myself to speak to the owners. I was thinking what to say when a short, pretty woman with a bright pink face popped up in front of me. "How may I help you?"

"Are you Mia Willow?" I asked hopefully.

She looked surprised. "Yes. I've seen you before, haven't I?"

I nodded. "Yes, my friend Matilda and I sometimes buy products here, but my twin sister Rebecca owns the cupcake store not far from here."

"Rebecca!" she said with a wide smile. "Did you say you and Rebecca were twins? Surely you're not identical twins, because you don't look anything like each other."

"We are identical twins," I said, "but she is Amish and I left the Amish years ago. I'm sure if I dressed Amish, I'd look just like her."

Mia simply smiled and nodded. She shot me an expectant look, so I pushed on. "I suppose you've heard that Colin Greaves died in my sister's store?"

"Hello?"

I looked up to see William. A burly man, he was as tall and well built as his wife was short and slim. "Are you talking about Colin Greaves?"

I nodded again. "He died in my sister's store."

William nodded vigorously. "Yes, dreadful business." He tut-tutted.

Matilda butted in. "Well, Mr. Greaves died *after* the paramedics took him from the store, but he collapsed *in* the store."

I was quite nervous and so I lost my train of thought, as I do when I'm nervous. "Oh, um, he was poisoned," I sputtered.

"Yes, I heard that," Mia said.

"We were told it was a poisonous herb that did him in," Matilda said. "The police suspect you and Rebecca because you were the only ones holding out, refusing to sell to Colin Greaves. That makes both of you suspects in the eyes of the police."

I expected William and Mia to look shocked at Matilda's blunt words, but they didn't. Mia sighed. "Yes, William and I had to go downtown and make a statement," she said. "Then the police came here and looked through all our herbs and confiscated some of them."

"Which ones did they confiscate?" I asked her.

She shrugged one shoulder. "I don't rightly remember. Do you, William?"

He shook his head. "They gave me a list. They said we would get them all back, so I wasn't too concerned."

"They took all Rebecca's cupcakes and we certainly won't get those back," I said indignantly.

"That's not fair," Mia said. "He was definitely murdered then? It wasn't on the news."

I was surprised at that. "Wasn't it? I rarely watch the news since it's usually always bad news."

"I watch the news and I didn't see it either," Matilda said.

"Maybe the police withheld it for a reason," I said, wondering what the reason could be. "Anyway, I'm worried because I'm sure the police see me as the main suspect and I was wondering if you'd have any idea who could have killed him?"

"It wasn't us if that's what you're thinking," Mia said with a chuckle. "Sure, we do sell some Traditional Chinese Medicine herbs, but we have to have a letter from a practitioner before we release them. We don't just sell anything poisonous to the public at large. We are quite careful."

"Did the police give you the third degree about all that?" I asked her.

She nodded. "They sure did!"

"Did Colin Greaves ever threaten you?" I asked her. "Just before he collapsed, he threatened Rebecca, but it wasn't an overt threat as such, more of a veiled threat. Still, he made quite sure we knew it was a threat."

"Was it just before he collapsed?" Mia's eyes narrowed.

"Yes. Did he threaten you at all?"

"He threatened us on a regular basis," she said, raising her eyebrows. "But it was like you said—it was always a veiled threat. He never said he would burn down the building or break our legs. " She broke off with a chuckle. "Still, he always said it would be better for us if we sold, and he always worded it in such a way that if it was repeated, it wouldn't sound bad at all."

I nodded. "I know exactly what you mean. That's how he was that day."

"He came in here just before he went to Rebecca's store, didn't he William?" Mia said. "I wasn't here at the time. I was in the back room doing orders."

"That's right," William said. "He didn't stay as long as usual, less than five minutes. He used to go on at length, but this time he was quite brief."

"Did he make you a higher offer?"

Both of them looked surprised. "Did he make *you* a higher offer?" Mia asked me.

"Yes, he made Rebecca a significantly higher offer. Didn't he make you one too?"

"Yes he did," William said.

"And did he threaten you again?"

William shook his head. "This time I told him I would give the offer serious consideration. It was much more than we would get if we put the place on the market. It was a very good price. Very tempting, in fact."

Maybe Colin Greaves had thought he was on a winner. Maybe that's why he had not taken his usual length of time in their store that day. "Do you mind me asking why you didn't accept his previous offers?"

Mia was the one who answered. "Because we didn't really have anywhere else to go. We like it here. We've been here for years and we're quite comfortable here. If we go somewhere else, we will have to start from scratch and neither of us wanted to go through the hassle."

William interrupted her. "Still, his latest offer sweetened it."

I noticed a customer was hanging around

wanting to speak with William and Mia, so I said, "Thanks for your help. Please come over to Rebecca's store if you think of anything else. It's not nice being a suspect."

"Sure," they both said before turning to the customer.

Matilda and I walked out into the street. When we were out of earshot, Matilda said to me, "What did you make of that?"

"I don't know. We only have her husband's word for it that he was thinking of accepting Greaves's offer. I thought Mia looked surprised when he said it."

Matilda nodded sagely. "Yes, that's exactly what I was thinking. If they murdered Greaves, they had enough time to slip him the poison and that fits with the timeframe given that the vic went to Rebecca's store next. Then the husband could simply pretend to the police that he was accepting Greaves's offer."

"Something else occurred to me," I told her. "I'm wondering if the Willows were holding out for a higher price. What if they did intend to sell all along, but they knew that when there were only two or so stores left that Greaves would increase his offer to a nice sum."

"But then they wouldn't have murdered him," Matilda said.

I clutched my head with both hands. This was all terribly confusing.

Just as I made to walk into Rebecca's store, the hair stood up on the back of my neck. I had that watched feeling again. I spun around, just in time to see a figure duck behind the building. I grabbed Matilda's arm. "Did you see that?"

She looked around her. "What?"

"You know how I said I was being followed? I saw him just over there." I pointed.

"So it's a man?"

"Actually, I suppose it could have been a woman," I said. "I didn't get a good look at him or her."

Matilda dragged me away from the shop door and into the apartment entrance. "I don't like this, Jane. I don't like it at all. Someone's been following you, and Colin Greaves collapsed in Rebecca's store and then died. What if you're next?"

CHAPTER 12

"And so I've become used to being alone," I lamented, although I suspected my audience was not the least interested in what I had to say. "Even when I was married, I spent most of my time alone. My husband was really never home, but knowing that there is someone living in the house, at least officially, is different from being completely alone."

I looked around the living room. "I've only known Eleanor and Matilda a short time, but already they feel like family. I half wished I'd gone with them to their indoor rock climbing lesson, but it is their thing and I didn't want to intrude. And there's the fact that I wouldn't last a minute trying something like that. Now I'm home alone, and it's not like it was last week when I would have been happy. I feel restless. Maybe it's because I'm a suspect in a murder investigation. Maybe it's because my ex-husband and his much, much, *much* younger new bride already have a baby and I've never had one."

I walked into the kitchen, snatched a tissue from the box, and dabbed at my eyes. I turned around. "Am I making any sense?" I threw both hands into the air.

Mr. Crumbles looked at me, meowed, and stalked toward his food bowl.

"At least you have your priorities right," I said, scooping some food into his bowl. "They say talking to yourself is the first sign of madness, so I wonder what they say about talking to a cat?"

The little cat continued to eat.

I just had to get out of the apartment. The café nearby was open quite late, so I decided to walk there and have some coffee. I'd eaten much earlier with Matilda and Eleanor, but now I needed some air.

And so, fifty minutes later I was sitting in the café sipping my second cup of coffee. I was sure I wouldn't be getting any sleep that night.

"Miss Delight."

I nearly jumped out of my skin. I looked up from the liquid depths of my coffee into the ruggedly handsome face of Detective McCloud. My first thought was that he was there to arrest me. "What do you want?" I said in alarm.

"I'm not here on official business," he said.

I tried not to look too relieved. "No, of course not," I said.

"Are you here alone?" he asked me.

"Yes I am," I said, wondering why he was asking.

"I thought your friends might be with you."

"Eleanor and Matilda? No, they've gone to their indoor rock climbing lesson."

Detective McCloud chuckled. "They are most interesting ladies. What are you doing here?"

I wondered why he was asking me. I narrowed my eyes. "I come here on occasion."

"Do you mind if I join you?"

"Please do." I really wanted to say, "No, go away," because I was afraid he would question me.

He sat down and ordered coffee too.

"I'm on my second," I told him when the waitress left. "It's decaf but I'm sure there's still enough caffeine to keep me up all night."

"Is there something worrying you?" he asked.

"Other than being a suspect in a murder case?" I let my words hang on the air.

The detective shrugged one shoulder. "I didn't say you were."

"Well, it's obvious, isn't it?" I said.

He did not respond, but instead said, "Do you mind if I ask you some questions about the Amish?"

A wave of relief hit me. So that's why he was here. He simply wanted information and he wasn't here because I was a murder suspect. I exhaled slowly. "I was Amish until I went on *rumspringa*."

"I've been trying to read up on the Amish since I arrived here but haven't had much of a chance to do so. *Rumspringa*. I'm pretty sure I know what that means."

"Most Amish communities have *rumspringa*. It's when a young person leaves the community to experience English—oh, that's non-Amish—ways. If they want to return to the Amish, then they do and they get baptized."

"So they aren't baptized as babies?"

I shook my head. "No. Amish are Anabaptists. They believe in someone making a decision for baptism."

He nodded slowly. "I see. And if someone goes on *rumspringa* and doesn't return, are they shunned?"

I laughed. "No, that's a common misconception. I didn't return after my *rumspringa* and I certainly wasn't shunned. Anyway, someone has to be baptized before they can be shunned. You can't shun someone who hasn't been baptized. I was never baptized into the Amish community. Besides, not returning from *rumspringa* is certainly not a valid reason to be shunned."

"This is most helpful," he said. "I was told there is such a big Amish community here that I have to find out about their ways."

"But you see, Amish are very law-abiding citizens," I told him. "You really won't find Amish committing any crimes." I narrowed my eyes as I said it. I hope he took the hint that Rebecca certainly couldn't have murdered anyone.

Once more, he did not respond to my words, but asked, "Can you recommend a good book for me to learn about the Amish?"

"Well, there are a few," I said, "but the thing is, every community is different. What would be normal for one community would not be for another. Plus, every community goes by the Ordnung."

"Could you spell that?"

I spelled it and then added, "The Ordnung is basically an unwritten set of rules that every community has. It governs things like the type of dress permitted, restrictions on the type of buggy allowed, the technologies people can't own but can maybe use, that sort of thing. Like I said, it's different in every community."

"And the language the Amish speak. Is it Dutch? I can speak some French but that's about all."

I chuckled. "No, Pennsylvania Dutch really is Pennsylvania *Deutsche*. At least that's what most people think. It's German, but it's a dialect of German."

The detective's coffee arrived and he stirred a considerable amount of sugar into it. I must have stared because he looked up and laughed. "One of the drawbacks of my job, I'm afraid. I need instant energy. That, and I have a sweet tooth."

I laughed too. "You and me both." My imagination ran away with me and I wondered what it would be like sitting there on a date with the detective. I was fifty going on fifty-one, and I had thought any chance for love was well and truly over.

The detective drank his coffee quickly and then said, "Thanks for the information, Miss Delight. You've been most helpful." With that, he hurried away from the table.

So much for imagining being on a date with someone like him! He had gotten his information and left soon after. My spirits fell. I decided to go home. Despite the coffee, I was feeling tired and thought I should get some sleep. I hadn't had much the previous night.

As I walked out the door, I saw Detective McCloud speaking with some men. I figured they were off duty police officers. I looked the other way so I wouldn't have to speak to him and walked out the door. I had only gotten about five paces when I saw a shadow opposite.

A chill ran through me. I had been sure someone was following me, so why had I been so silly as to come out alone at night?

I didn't know what to do, so I stood there frozen to the spot, staring at the place where I had seen someone. Just then, the moon came out from behind the clouds and I saw the moonlight reflecting on something, maybe a watch, where I had seen the figure.

I turned and hurried back into the café.

Detective McCloud stopped speaking to his friends and looked up. "Miss Delight! Is something wrong? You're as white as a sheet."

"There's someone out there," I said.

He stepped away from the other men and towered over me. "What do you mean?"

"I know it sounds silly, but lately I've been sure someone is following me, and just then when I went to walk home, I saw someone duck back behind a building."

"Come outside with me and point out the building to me."

I did as he asked.

"Now, Miss Delight, I want you to go back inside and wait for me."

I hurried back into the café. Just before I went inside, I looked over my shoulder and saw the detective running across the street.

I stood just inside the café waiting for him to come back. It wasn't long before he did so. "I didn't catch him. He was too far away," he said.

"Did you see him?" I said in surprise.

"Someone was running away and had too much of a start on me," he said. "There's no need to alarm yourself, Miss Delight. It might be nothing to do with you. When did you first notice this?"

"It was several weeks ago," I said.

"And have you been able to get a good look at the person?"

I shook my head. "No, not at all. I've only seen a figure ducking behind the buildings, that sort of thing. The last time was earlier today when we came back from Sarah Beiler's house."

"I'll walk you home now," Detective McCloud said. "Look, would you do me a favor and not go out after dark? It's probably nothing to worry about, so it's just to be on the safe side. Don't go anywhere alone, at least not until I make some inquiries."

"Thanks," I said, and I was grateful, but I did not know what sort of inquiries he could make.

The detective walked me to the door to my apartment and then said, "I'll wait until you're safely inside. Immediately lock the door behind me." He pulled out his card and handed it to me. "That has my direct cell phone number on it. If you hear anything or see anything and you are at all worried, don't hesitate to call me, even if you think it's something insignificant."

I thanked him once more, let myself inside and then locked the door. I leaned back against the door, shaking. I knew it hadn't been my imagination. I knew someone had been following me and Detective McCloud had seen him or her. What's more, he seemed to think I might be in danger.

Who could it be, and why was someone interested in little old me?

CHAPTER 13

The following morning, I was sitting in my car, and Matilda was driving. That was a concern in itself, but worse still, I was dressed in my sister's Amish clothes—a prayer *kapp*, a dress, a black apron, black stockings, and sensible shoes. My hair was pulled back, parted in the middle, and twisted into a bun.

My hair was not as long as my sister's hair. Of course, my sister had never cut hers, as was the Amish way. I used to have mine short, but after I divorced I hadn't bothered going to a hairstylist to have it cut. At least it gave me more of an authentic Amish look, as it was long enough to tuck up under the prayer *kapp*.

"Do you think this is going to work?" Matilda asked doubtfully.

"How should I know?" I said, throwing my hands into the air. "It wasn't my idea; it was yours."

"Well, it sounded like a good idea at the time," Matilda admitted, "but now I'm not so sure."

"No, it really does sound like a good idea to me. I'm sure you're right—Greaves's wife Stephanie will be more inclined to speak with me if she thinks I'm Amish and she thinks you're my driver. It *is* a good idea," I said again, more to reassure myself than anything else.

"Have you decided what you're going to say?" Matilda asked me.

I rubbed my eyes with both hands. "Vaguely, but if I think about it too much, my mind will go blank. I'll play it by ear."

Matilda snorted. "You mean you'll make it up as you go along."

I chuckled. "Pretty much."

"As we agreed, you do all the talking, but don't forget to find out if anyone else inherits the money. We are just assuming it's only Stephanie and her son Brooks, but for all we know there could be other siblings. Specifically ask if they're aware of the terms of the will, because Greaves might have left something to his mistress."

I shook my finger at Matilda. "There you go again, talking about his mistress. What makes you think he had a mistress?"

Matilda swerved violently, I assume to miss something on the road. Whether there was something on the road or she imagined it, I had no idea because I shut my eyes tightly and gripped the seat for dear life. "You do have a driver's license, don't you?" I asked.

"Of course I do! I got an international license in Kochkor-Ata."

I had no idea where that was, and was too scared to ask. "Would you mind slowing down a bit please, Matilda? There's no rush! And besides, we don't want to attract the attention of the police."

"Oh, sorry." Matilda really did sound contrite. "For a minute I thought I was back in northern India, scurrying around those mountain roads. You know, it's quite easy to pop over the edge there. You see trucks over cliff edges all the time. I laugh when people say mountain roads are dangerous here because they've never been to northern India. Why, I could tell you stories!"

I had no doubt she could. "Um, have you ever driven over a cliff edge?" I asked her.

Matilda shot me a look of disgust. "Of course not! Oh, there was that one incident when I was on my way to celebrate New Year's Eve in the White Desert…" She didn't finish her sentence, because majestic brass gates loomed in front of us. "What are we going to do?" she asked in alarm.

"They're clearly open a little bit, so they're certainly not locked. What if I get out and push them open?"

"Are you out of your mind, Jane? We are supposed to talk into some intercom device and announce ourselves and ask to be let in. You can't simply go to those gates and open them."

At least that's what I think she said, because I was already half way to the gates before she finished speaking. I gave one gate a tentative push and it swung open. I turned around and gave Matilda the thumbs up and then pushed both gates wide open. In case there were cameras trained on me, I walked in a sedate manner back to the car. "Let's go," I said.

Matilda clutched her stomach.

"Are you all right?"

"Not really," she said. "I feel scared walking into a murderer's lair."

"Do you think Stephanie did it?" I asked her.

"I don't really know," she said. "In Agatha Christie novels it's never the obvious one, and Stephanie is the obvious one because she stands to inherit. Maybe though she was in it with his mistress, or maybe she was in it with both his mistress and his mistress's husband."

I rubbed my eyes again, and then stopped myself. It would cause wrinkles, more wrinkles than I already had. Things were rapidly going downhill. "Let's just see what facts we can uncover," I said.

Matilda stopped at the front door. I looked up at the big house. When I was married to Ted, we lived in a big house, but it was only half the size of this house. Colin Greaves must have been worth millions, and then some.

"Do we knock on the door?" Matilda asked me. "What if the butler answers and turns us away?"

"There might not be a butler," I said, "but we won't know unless we try."

I tried to walk in a sedate manner once more in case someone was watching. Matilda knocked on the door. No one answered. We exchanged glances. Surely someone was home.

Matilda knocked again several times. Finally, a woman answered the door. She was quite haughty, and looked down her nose at us. Waves of no doubt very expensive perfume preceded her. "What do you want?" she said in a curt tone.

"Are you Stephanie Greaves?" I asked her.

The woman narrowed her eyes at me. "Yes?" She spoke with her lips barely parted, I fancied like a snake hissing.

"I'm Rebecca Yoder, and this is my driver, Matilda Birtwistle," I said. "I do hope you don't mind me coming to speak with you, but your husband passed away in my cupcake store."

The woman's eyes widened and she appeared to be struggling with some inner dialogue. Finally, she said, "Do come in, won't you. I'll have Celia fetch us a drink."

She showed us through an opulent foyer into a lavish living room. French antiques were dotted all about the foyer, an abundance of gilded tulipwood and oak veneer with delicate renderings of amaranth and holly, as well as Aubusson silk sofa chairs. I recognized the furniture as Louis XIV as my ex-husband's mother collected French antiques.

The living room stood in stark contrast to the foyer. It was as minimalist as the foyer was luxurious. Everything was white, from the massive chandelier to the grand piano. Nothing was out of place, and I didn't see any sign of a pet. If I had, I am sure it would have been white. For the first time I noticed Stephanie Greaves was dressed in a smart white skirt and matching blouse, with a single strand of pearls.

A gray-haired woman entered the room. Stephanie at once barked at her. "Celia, fetch everybody a drink, won't you." To us she said, "What would you like?"

"I'd like some strong coffee, please," Matilda said.

"Would you happen to have lemonade?" I asked.

"And I'll have my usual." Stephanie dismissed a clearly harried Celia with a wave of her hand. Celia scurried from the room.

"I shall be upfront with you and tell you that my husband and I were not on the best of terms," Stephanie said, "yet I am totally devastated about his passing." Her eyes lit up as she said it and I sincerely doubted she was devastated in the least.

"Yes, it was most sad," I said. "He collapsed in my store and I, I mean my sister Jane, tended to him while I called 911. The paramedics came awfully fast, but alas, they were not able to save him."

"Yes, the police said he was poisoned," she said.

I wondered if she thought we had poisoned him, so I added, "Yes. I believe he was poisoned at least fifteen minutes before he entered my store."

I noticed a flicker of surprise when I said that, so maybe the police hadn't told her. "I see," she said slowly. She bit her nail. As her hands were perfectly manicured, I figured she didn't bite her nails often.

Celia hurried into the room and placed the drinks in front of everyone. It looked as though Stephanie had some sort of cocktail. My lemonade was served in sparkling crystal, and Matilda's coffee in fine bone china.

"May I speak freely? I don't want to cause any offense or bring back upsetting memories," I said, stumbling over my words.

"Yes, say whatever you like." Stephanie leaned forward.

"I am most distressed that your husband passed away in my store, or well, shortly afterwards," I said. "The police don't seem to have any clue who murdered him, and I was wondering if you'd have any idea?"

"Why? What's it to you?" she asked. "I mean, why would you be interested in who killed him?"

I lowered my eyes and spoke slowly. "It is our ways, you understand. I feel the weight of responsibility because he collapsed in my store. It would put my mind at rest if you could list all his enemies and then I can devote myself to praying for them." I hoped it didn't sound as far-fetched to Stephanie as it did to me. *Please forgive me for that terrible lie,* I silently prayed.

If Stephanie did not believe me, she showed no sign. "Oh yes, of course," she said. "I do admire the Amish ways, how you all live a life of simplicity and faith. It must be wonderful."

"Yes, I am most blessed," I said. "Now if you could give me the list of people who had something against him? Then I can pray for them to see the error of their ways and turn about. 'All we like sheep have turned astray; we have turned every one to his own way, and the Lord hath laid on him the iniquity of us all'," I quoted. In my former community, anyone who quoted Scripture would likely be chastized for showing off their knowledge of Scripture in public, but I knew Stephanie wouldn't know enough about the Amish to be surprised I quoted Scripture.

"Well, there's his mistress, of course."

Matilda coughed violently. "Are you all right?" Stephanie asked her.

"Yes, yes." She waved one hand. "The coffee went down the wrong way."

I was genuinely shocked. "A mistress? Your husband had a mistress? And you know about the mistress?"

"Well Colin didn't know that I knew, of course," she said. "I had a private detective following him around. I told the police, and I know you ladies won't tell anyone."

I did my best to process the information. "And you think his mistress might have killed him?"

She nodded. "Perhaps. I mean they had been seeing each other for some time and I guess she wanted my husband to divorce me for her. This is all pure speculation, you understand. I told the police all this, so if there is any truth to it, they'll find out."

"Didn't you mind that he had a mistress?" I asked her, my curiosity getting the better of me.

"Well, yes and no," she said. "I haven't been in love with my husband for years, but we did have a comfortable life." She broke off and gestured around the room. "We both signed an airtight pre-nup before we married, so neither of us could leave or we would lose everything. He never bothered me. I did my own thing and I didn't really care whether he was here or not. He was welcome to his mistress as far as I could care. The only thing is I thought it quite rude of him."

"Yes, I am terribly sorry," I said. "Do you have her name, so I can pray for her?"

Matilda whipped a notepad and pen from her pocket.

"Iris. Iris Ogilvie," Stephanie said.

"Yes, I will pray for her." And I really would have to—I could not bring myself to say I would pray for someone and then not do so.

"And did his mistress have a husband?" Matilda asked. "Rebecca here would need to pray for him too."

"Yes, I will definitely need to pray for him."

"Richard is his name," Stephanie said. "I haven't met either of them, of course, but the private investigator did give me a file on them with their photos. I gave the file to the police, of course."

"That's most helpful. Thank you so much. I'll pray for both of them. And would you mind if I prayed for you as well in your time of need?" I quickly amended that to, "I know you're not exactly in need, but it must be a trying time for you."

"Yes it is. Thank you for praying for me. That's nice of you."

I nodded to Matilda and she wrote something on her notepad.

"And do you have any children? I'd like to pray for them as they lost their father."

Stephanie nodded, causing light to reflect from her huge diamond earrings. "We have the one child, my son Brooks."

"He must be such a comfort to you," I said. "Is he coming back to town for the funeral?"

"Oh, he lives here," Stephanie said. "In this house. Or rather he did, until…" her voice trailed away. After an interval, she added, "And he's recently moved back home, to the pool house out back. It's next to the pool," she said, somewhat unnecessarily.

I turned to Matilda. "Matilda, would you mind writing his name as well?" To Stephanie, I said, "Did your husband have any other relatives I should pray for?"

"No, just the two of us."

I tapped my chin. "Oh goodness me. Something just occurred to me."

Once more, Stephanie leaned forward. "What is it?"

"Oh dear me, it's not polite of me to say, but what if your husband left something to his mistress in the will? Then that would give her a motive to murder him and I would have to pray even harder."

Stephanie frowned. "That occurred to me too, but I've already been in touch with the lawyer. No, Brooks and I are the only ones who inherit."

"Did I hear my name mentioned?"

I looked up at the owner of the softly spoken drawl. I knew at once this was Stephanie's son Brooks as he was dressed all in white, matching both his mother and the room in which he was now standing.

His mother made the introductions and Brooks inclined his head and offered a slight nod. He walked to the bar and poured himself a brandy and then took a seat on an antique giltwood chair near his mother, facing us.

"And these ladies were with your father when he passed," Stephanie said, ending the introductions.

"Actually, I wasn't. Jane, I mean Rebecca here was," Matilda said.

I spoke up. "Yes. I'm sorry to tell you that

your father passed away in my cupcake store. My sister went to his aid. I called 911, but it was too late."

"That's too bad," Brooks said, averting his eyes.

He was softly spoken, and I could see his hands were soft. I doubted he had done a hard day's work in his life. In fact, I would be surprised if he had done a hard five minute's work in his life. It also seemed he had either very good sunscreen or he spent all his life indoors.

"I'm very sorry for your loss," I continued.

Brooks again gave me a half nod. "Thank you. It's kind of you to come. Is that why you've come, to offer your condolences?"

"That's right," I said, "and to pray."

Brooks raised his eyebrows. "For whom?"

"Well, for you and your mother, of course," Matilda said, "and for anyone else who would be affected by your father's passing."

"I'm sure Dad's mistress was affected by his passing," Brooks said, his voice dripping with sarcasm.

Stephanie shot him a sharp look. "Brooks!"

He looked down at his white leather shoes. "Sorry."

"I'll pray for her too, and I'll pray for anyone

else who would be saddened by your father's passing."

"This kind lady is going to pray for your father's enemies as well," Stephanie said to Brooks.

Brooks looked startled. "For his enemies? Why would you do that?"

I couldn't think of a ready answer, so I decided to offer another Scripture. "He maketh His sun to rise on the evil and the good, and sendeth rain on the just and on the unjust," I said. Brooks looked at me blankly so I added, "Pray for them which despitefully use you."

I thought the Scriptures most useful, but Stephanie yawned widely and said in a bored tone, "It's most kind of you to pray for everyone."

I looked directly at Brooks. "Would you have any idea who might have murdered your father?"

If he had thought such a question too forthright for an Amish lady to ask, he showed no sign. "Well, lots of people. His mistress, his mistress's husband, and no doubt the people he was in business with. Dad made a lot of enemies. He stepped on a lot of toes."

"Brooks!" Stephanie said again.

"Well, I shall pray for them all," I said. "It's very sad, isn't it, and it must be unpleasant for you with the police poking around. They've taken me in for questioning as well and it was most distressing."

Brooks's jaw fell open. "They took you in for questioning? Why would they do that? You're Amish!"

"Your father had eaten one of my sample cupcakes, and they thought that might have been what poisoned him so they questioned me," I told him. "However, they soon found out that other customers ate the cupcakes and those customers are unaffected."

"Do the detectives still suspect you?" Brooks asked.

I shook my head. "No, not since the police found out that your father was poisoned at least fifteen minutes before he entered my store."

Brooks rubbed his chin. "Fifteen minutes you say?" He looked off at a large painting hanging over the white marble fireplace. The painting too was white, although it had faint touches of color. From where I was sitting I couldn't quite make out what it was.

I took the opportunity to study Brooks. He had thick, long hair, the type worn by televangelists in the 1980s and the early 1990s. He used liberal amounts of aftershave, or maybe it was men's cologne. Whatever it was, the heady scent of spices and vanilla hung in a thick cloud around him. I looked at the fingers clutching a brandy glass and his nails were perfectly manicured.

I wondered if he could be the poisoner. After all, he didn't look as though he had the stomach to strangle anyone and I figured poison would be his weapon of choice.

"Given that your father drove himself to my store and also the neighboring store of William and Mia Willow," I began, "it stands to reason that there must have been someone in the car with him when he was poisoned."

"I wonder if someone had given him poisoned coffee," Brooks said, looking thoughtful.

Matilda shrugged. "As you would know, the police impounded his car and searched it. I suspect that someone was in the car with him and they administered the poison in some sort of substance and then took the remains away."

"I wonder what it could have been in?" Brooks said. "Maybe they slipped something into his coffee."

I made a mental note to ask Wanda Hershberger to find out from her daughter. Even if they couldn't tell what substance the poison had been in, they would definitely know the contents of his stomach.

"The police questioned us as well," Brooks offered, "given that my mother and I inherit."

"I'm sure the police always look at who inherits first," Matilda said.

Brooks looked at her as though he was seeing her for the first time. "Quite so," he said. "Mom was worried that Dad's mistress might inherit something and the lawyer said she didn't."

There was a sharp intake of breath from Stephanie's direction, and I figured she didn't want to admonish her son yet again in front of us. Clearly, she was not pleased by what he was saying.

I wanted to discover if Brooks had an alibi, but I had no idea of the right questions to ask. I could hardly ask him where he was at the time of his father's murder. Instead, I said, "I expect the police are looking closely at everyone who doesn't have an alibi."

"Yes, that's probably where they lost interest in both of us," Stephanie said, gesturing to her son, then back to herself. "We were together binge watching episodes of *When Calls the Heart* on Netflix."

I didn't think Brooks would enjoy the Hallmark

channel as much as his mother, but of course an Amish lady wouldn't know that. I was grateful when Matilda spoke up. "I would not have thought that your type of show, Brooks?"

"I've been watching it with Mom to make her happy. It's not something I'd watch given the choice, but it makes Mom happy."

Stephanie shot Brooks a winning smile.

"What part of the show do you like the most?" I said, hoping to figure out whether or not he had actually watched it.

"I don't really like anything about it. It's more of a chick flick," he said. "I liked all those people who changed into creatures, but that's about it."

Stephanie gasped. "Brooks, there were no creatures! You have it mixed up with something else. Don't you remember? It was the show with the Mountie."

Brooks turned red. "Oh yes, I remember it now. The show with the Mountie."

I wondered if Stephanie had cooked up a scheme with her son to give them both an alibi. If so, she should have counseled him to pretend he liked the show and told him what it was about.

"I've watched *When Calls the Heart*," Matilda said. "I very much enjoyed it too."

The questions were getting us nowhere. Brooks and Stephanie alleged they had an alibi. Something occurred to me. "Was anyone else here watching the show with you?" I asked Brooks.

"Why do you want to know?" he asked in a belligerent manner.

"No, it was just the two of us," Stephanie said in even tones. "Brooks was keeping me company. It was so good of him to watch something I'd like to see. I couldn't really watch those action movies that he likes to watch. Entirely too unsettling, you understand."

I nodded slowly. So no one else was with them and they had given each other an alibi, which to my thinking ruled their alibis out. Matilda shot me a strange look. I knew she was thinking exactly the same thing, that Stephanie and Brooks were in it together.

"Oh that's good," I said. "Is there anyone else you can think of that we should pray for?"

"No, no one else," she said.

"Well, I'm very sorry for your loss and all the hassles it brings you," I said. I stood up, as did Matilda.

"I grow my own herbal remedies," Matilda told her. "My sister Eleanor and I lived just out of

Dalian in China for some years and we became interested in Traditional Chinese Medicine. I noticed you have some young ginkgo biloba trees growing at the front of your house."

Stephanie's face changed. For once, she looked truly interested. "I was a Traditional Chinese Medicine practitioner before I met my husband. That's actually how we met. He was a client of mine."

I wondered if the police knew that. It sounded awfully incriminating to me. Stephanie would know all about wolfsbane in that case.

"That's wonderful," Matilda said. "My sister and I grow a vast array of herbs. Do you still grow your own?"

Stephanie clasped her hands in delight. "Yes I do."

"Oh, may I have a quick peek at your garden?"

Stephanie's expression changed. She looked quite put out. I thought she would refuse. After hesitating for what seemed an age, she finally said, "I can show you quickly, but then I must take my leave because I have an appointment with my lawyer."

"A quick look would be lovely," Matilda said.

"It's so wonderful to meet someone else who is interested in Traditional Chinese Medicine."

Stephanie led us through a huge kitchen with sparkling granite countertops to an extensive herb garden just behind the kitchen.

Stephanie waved one hand over it. "Well, there you go!"

"You have such a wonderfully extensive herb garden," Matilda said. "It puts mine to shame."

Celia appeared at Stephanie's shoulder.

"It was so kind of you ladies to come and offer to pray for me," Stephanie said. "Celia will show you to your car."

"Oh, thanks so much, goodbye," I said.

Celia marched around the edge of the building, and ushered us along a white gravel path to where the car was parked. She stood there with her arms crossed, as another car approached. My hand was reaching for the car door when a familiar figure jumped out of the car.

"Mrs. Yoder, Mrs. Birtwistle," the voice called.

I stood, frozen to the spot. Detective McCloud! Would he recognize me? I wished I was wearing a bonnet over my prayer *kapp* so I could pull it over my face.

He strode over to us. "What are you ladies doing here?" His tone was accusatory.

Matilda spoke up. "Rebecca wanted to come and pray for Mrs. Greaves," she told him. She looked as though butter wouldn't melt in her mouth.

"That's right," I said, looking down the detective's shoes. "It is our ways. The poor man died in my store, or at least collapsed in my store, so I need to pray for all his relatives." I knew Detective McCloud wouldn't know any better. I felt bad for deceiving him.

He put his hands on his hips. "Is that so?"

I thought it best to speak in Pennsylvania Dutch. " En Schtich in Zeit is neine wart schpaeder naus." He stared at me, so I added, "Ich hab en aker grummbiere geblanst."

"Quite so," he said. "Well, good day, ladies. I must go and speak with Mrs. Greaves." With that, he strode away.

I wasted no time getting in the car. "That was a close call," I said. "Matilda, do you think he recognized me?"

"No I don't. You *are* identical twins and you do look just like Rebecca in those clothes," Matilda said. "I think it was doubtful for a moment, but when you spoke in Pennsylvania Dutch that confused him. I don't know why, since you can speak Pennsylvania Dutch too. Maybe that didn't occur to him at the time."

"I hope it doesn't occur to him later," I said, wincing.

"Anyway, what did you say to him?"

I chuckled. "I said the first expressions that came to my head even though they make no sense."

Matilda laughed. She hit the gas and I was flung back in my seat. "What did you say?" she asked again.

I told her. "'A stitch in time, saves nine,' and then I said, 'I planted an acre of potatoes.'"

Matilda laughed but then stopped abruptly. "You know, Jane, there was wolfsbane growing in Stephanie's herb garden."

CHAPTER 14

"Stephanie did it for sure," Eleanor said. "She doesn't have any pets. That means she can't be trusted."

Matilda rolled her eyes. "What a silly thing to say, Eleanor! Lots of nice people don't have pets. Someone might be allergic to pets and so can't have any. There are plenty of reasons. Besides, everyone who doesn't have pets isn't a murderer."

Eleanor folded her arms.

"Stephanie and her son will inherit a lot of money," I told Matilda, Eleanor, and Rebecca.

"I don't think the police are looking too hard at them," Rebecca said.

I was puzzled. "What makes you think that?"

"The detectives were around here earlier today."

I was shocked. "Why didn't you tell me?"

"I didn't want to worry you," Rebecca said. "I was going to tell you after work, and I just did."

I rubbed my eyes. "Both detectives? I told you I ran into Detective McCloud when I was pretending to be you."

Rebecca pulled a face. "I hope you didn't do anything to embarrass me."

"I doubt it. I hope not. I don't think I did," I said.

"No, she acted just like you," Matilda said with a chuckle.

Rebecca was clearly at a loss as to how to take that. Finally, she said, "No, it was that other detective. What's his name, Stirling?"

"What did he want?" I asked her.

"He told me none of the cakes were poisoned."

"But that's not news," Eleanor exclaimed, extracting one of Mr. Crumbles' claws from her leg. "The poor thing. He hasn't learned how to retract his claws yet."

"Yes, I expect the detective was just trying to snoop around," Rebecca said.

I was exasperated. "But what could he hope to find? And did he know you were not me?"

Of course, the two of us had swapped clothes.

Rebecca chuckled. "I'm glad the bishop didn't catch me! I haven't worn English clothes since I was on *rumspringa* all those years ago. No, I don't think he asked me where I was. I mean where you were— you know what I mean. I said you were out. I didn't elaborate and he didn't push it."

"But what could they possibly hope to find by snooping?" Eleanor asked.

I shook my head. "I don't know, but I don't like it. It makes me quite uneasy, to be honest. Detective McCloud was at Stephanie's house today so maybe they do in fact suspect her."

"But Stephanie has an ironclad alibi," Matilda offered. She tapped her chin. "If you ask me, Stephanie and Brooks have given each other an alibi. They would do that if they were in it together. And if Brooks did it, then Stephanie would give him an alibi. If Stephanie did it, then Brooks would give her an alibi."

"We do have the other suspects though," I pointed out, "and Stephanie said she had given the private detective's files to the police and said they know all about Greaves's mistress, Iris, and her husband Richard Ogilvie."

Rebecca raised her eyebrows. "The mistress?"

"Exactly."

"You know, I'm surprised Detective McCloud didn't give us a lecture today about not investigating the case," Matilda said. "Maybe he really did believe our story."

Rebecca put her hands over her ears. "Don't tell me any more. It's best if I don't know. But I really don't think we should trade places again, Jane."

"Sure," I said. I couldn't think of a reason why I would need to, at least not in the near future.

"What do we do next?" Matilda said.

"My next move is going home and seeing to dinner," Rebecca said. "Good night everyone. I'll be on my way."

"I'll walk you to your buggy," I said. I had told Rebecca about the person following me, but she didn't seem to be alarmed. "It's all in God's hands," she had said.

I walked Rebecca to the buggy and watched her horse trot away. Suddenly, I realized that I was now alone. Fear gripped me. How could I have been so stupid? Detective McCloud had told me not to go out alone. Sure, it was broad daylight, but there were not many people around. I walked as fast as I could back to the apartment, shut the door, and then leaned back against it. I let out a long sigh of relief before hurrying up the stairs.

Matilda and Eleanor were bickering when I entered the room. "Something occurred to me," I said.

They both looked at me. "What is it?" they asked in unison.

"I'm wondering *how* someone got a fatal amount into Colin Greaves and I'm also wondering *when* someone got a fatal dose into him. As far as we know, he drove here alone, but we can't be certain. If someone gave him the fatal dose then they had to have given it to him in the car."

"How do you figure that?" Matilda asked me.

"Because William Willow said Greaves was in there less than five minutes. He was in Rebecca's store for about five minutes. It wouldn't take him long to get from the health food store to Rebecca's store. As the fatal dose was administered at least fifteen minutes before he collapsed, it means someone gave it to him before he went into the health food store."

"It had to be someone in the car with him," Eleanor said, standing up abruptly and startling Mr.

Crumbles. She immediately jumped down and scooped the cat into her arms, all the while making cooing sounds to him.

I looked at the little cat. "You know, he looks as though he's doubled in weight already in such a short time."

Matilda clapped her hands. "Attention please! Don't get sidetracked, Jane. I think you're onto something. Greaves didn't have a driver, did he?"

"No, because he was parked directly outside the shop and the police impounded his car."

Matilda nodded slowly. "That sounds more and more as though there was someone in the car with him and they made themselves scarce. Yes, it's likely that the murderer was in the car with him."

"Still, it could have been anyone," I said, "and we don't know everyone's alibis. So someone was in the car with him, gave him a fatal dose of poison, and then left in a hurry."

"Perhaps they gave it to him in coffee or maybe a cake," Eleanor said absently.

"He certainly had a sweet tooth," I told her. "I don't think he would have refused a nice cupcake. He seemed to have a voracious appetite and sometimes when he came into the store, he ate several sample cupcakes at once. It always annoyed me, but Rebecca never seemed to mind."

"That's because she's Amish," Eleanor said. "The Amish don't seem to mind anything. You must have been a nice person when you were young and Amish, Jane."

I was struck speechless, but Eleanor giggled. "Of course you're a nice person now. I didn't mean it how it came out. I just meant you must have been a tolerant person when you were Amish." She clapped her hand over her mouth.

"I'd stop talking if I were you," Matilda said. "Jane, what is our next move?"

"Ice cream," I said. "I think much better when I've had ice cream." I walked over to the refrigerator and took out a tub of salted caramel. "Would anyone else like some?"

"Yes, please," they both said.

Soon we were sitting around eating ice cream. "The next person we should look at is the mistress," I said, "although the police do have the file on her so if she was suspicious, surely they'd know."

Eleanor waved her finger at me. "If the police knew who did it, they wouldn't have spoken to Rebecca today. No, you're not off the hook yet,

Jane. Don't let your guard down. We need to investigate his mistress."

"But how can we possibly do that?" I asked her. "I can hardly dress in Amish clothes again—you heard Rebecca—and pretend I'm going to pray for her because her lover was murdered."

Both Matilda and Eleanor chuckled. "No, you can't do that," Matilda agreed.

"Then how can we investigate her?" I said. "You know, I'm completely at a loss with this one. We need to find out her alibi for the time of the murder. Even if I could speak to her, why would she tell me anything?"

Eleanor set down her spoon. "I know. Why don't you pretend you're a reporter?"

"She wouldn't want to be interviewed by a reporter," I said. "I'm sure her husband doesn't know she was having an affair with Colin Greaves, so she's not going to want to speak to a reporter."

"Oh yes." Eleanor looked crestfallen.

"It was a good idea nonetheless," I said in an encouraging tone. "Let's all come up with ideas even if they don't work out. It's better than sitting around not having any ideas at all."

"We should find out what she does for a living," Eleanor said. "Maybe that will help."

"How will it help?" Matilda asked her, sounding quite grumpy.

"Perhaps Iris is a hairstylist. If so, one of us could make an appointment with her. Or maybe she is a dentist and one of us could make an appointment with her."

I held up one hand, palm outward. "No, not me. You're on your own with that one."

Matilda had a faraway look in her eyes. "Or maybe she's an interior designer, and we could ask her to design the apartment, or maybe she's a realtor and we could pretend we are looking for a house, or maybe she cleans houses, and we could ask her to clean our apartment, or maybe she grooms pets and we could ask her to shampoo Mr. Crumbles."

Mr. Crumbles ran under the couch. "Don't be so silly, Matilda," Eleanor said. "You've scared Mr. Crumbles."

"You're the one who's silly, Eleanor," Matilda retorted. "That cat can't speak English!"

"But he can understand it," Eleanor snapped. "Cats don't like being bathed,"

I thought I had better say something in a hurry. "What a good idea," I said loudly. "We need to find out what she does."

"Oh, I've had a terrible thought," Matilda said. "What if she's not from around these parts? What if she's from California? Then I'll have to fly right across the country just to get information from her."

"Surely Greaves had the affair with someone closer to home," I said. "It would be more convenient for him. Yes, the more I think about it, the more I think that he would have a mistress who was close by."

"I do hope you're right," Matilda said. "We have done so much traveling lately. Now I just want to stay home."

Eleanor stood up. "I'll fetch the laptop." Soon she was tapping away on the keys. "We're in luck! There is an Iris Ogilvie who is a realtor in this town. That's much better than being a dentist!"

"You're telling me," I said in a heartfelt manner. "But is it the right Iris Ogilvie? Is there any way you can find out if her husband's name is Richard?"

"I should be able to." Eleanor's tone was full of confidence. "There's a big photo of her so I'll do a reverse image search." Only a few minutes later, she exclaimed, "Aha! There are a whole lot of photos of her and one is of her with a man. I'm just going to click on it now."

"Try not to keep us in so much suspense," Matilda said dryly.

"Yes. Her husband is Richard Ogilvie."

"Great work, Eleanor," I said. "I don't know how you did it! Fantastic. This won't be as bad as I thought. We can pretend we are looking for an apartment." I rubbed my hands together with glee. "Yes, this will work. We can casually mention we are looking for another apartment because a man collapsed here and later died."

"I have a good feeling about this," Matilda said.

"So do I," I said. "I'm so glad she's not a dentist. I certainly wouldn't want to have to make an appointment with a dentist just to question them about a murder suspect." I shut my eyes, having visions of lying in the dentist chair after asking questions of the dentist and the dentist looming over me with the drill. I shuddered and opened my eyes. "Show me the photo," I said. "I'm eager to know what she looks like."

I hurried over to look at the image of Iris Ogilvie, Greaves's mistress. "She isn't what I thought she'd look like, but then again, I didn't really have someone in mind. Whereas his wife has pale blonde hair and is all dressed in white, Iris is very colorful." In the photo, Iris was wearing quite garish clothes of every color of the rainbow. Her make-up looked as though it had been slapped on with a trowel. Stephanie looked as if she had swallowed several prunes, but Iris had a smiling, welcoming face.

"She doesn't look like a murderer," I added, "but what does a murderer actually look like?"

I absently walked to the other side of the room and looked out on the street below. I smiled as Detective McCloud's car was nowhere in sight. Maybe a small part of me was a little disappointed.

"I'll call her first thing in the morning and see if we can make an appointment with her for tomorrow," Matilda called across the room.

I made to turn, but as I did so, I noticed a man standing in front of the building opposite. I had not seen him at first because he was wearing dark clothes and was in the shadows. I pulled out my cell phone and called Detective McCloud.

CHAPTER 15

The previous night, Detective McCloud had sent over two uniformed officers. They hadn't found any one acting suspiciously, but Detective McCloud said the patrol car would scare away the perpetrator. He asked the patrol car to drive past on a regular basis.

Despite that, I had slept well, but now was quite anxious as Matilda had made an appointment with Iris Ogilvie. The three of us were going to pretend we were looking to buy a house in the hopes we would uncover something about her.

It was a long shot, but at least it was worth a try.

Eleanor and Matilda did not at all appear nervous when we met in the living room of the apartment. "You can leave all the talking to me,"

Matilda said in strident tones. "I have watched every Miss Marple movie there is. I know how to speak to suspects. I know exactly what to do."

Eleanor pulled a face. "How would Miss Marple try to fool a realtor?" she asked. Her expression was so earnest that I wondered if her question was serious.

"Don't be so literal, Eleanor," Matilda said, shooting her an angry look. "I know what to do. You wait and see."

I was a little worried, but what did I have to lose? Unless of course, Iris was the murderer and came after us. But even so, I thought that most unlikely.

Iris had wanted to collect us in her car, no doubt so we would be captive buyers, but Matilda had said we would meet her outside a café and go in her car from there.

Iris Ogilvie in person was every bit as colorful as her photo, although her smile in the photo had looked genuine. The smile on the woman's face as she walked toward us appeared to be anything but genuine. In fact, she seemed to have had so much plastic surgery, I wondered if the smile was frozen in place. Her skin was as tight as a drum, not a line in sight, and her lips were full and pouty.

"Doesn't she look great!" Eleanor said.

I nodded politely, wondering why Eleanor still had rollers in her hair. It appeared Iris was thinking the same thing, as she could not take her eyes off Eleanor's head. Finally she recovered and introduced herself.

Matilda smiled in response. "Lovely to meet you. I am Matilda Birtwistle. This is my sister, Eleanor Birtwistle, and this is our good friend, Jane Delight."

Iris appeared surprised at my name and I'm sure she would have raised her eyebrows had her face had the ability to do so. "That's an unusual name," she said.

I simply offered, "Yes it is."

"Now I have some wonderful properties to show you today, but aren't you looking to downsize?" She looked at Matilda and Eleanor as she said it and they both visibly bristled.

"Why on earth would we wish to downsize?" Matilda said, clearly irritated.

The realtor must have been a good enough judge of human nature to realize she had said the wrong thing. "Oh do forgive me, I meant upsize, of course," she said. "So you said the three of you are living in a small apartment now and you wish to move to a house?"

"It's a long story," Matilda said with a dismissive wave of her hand. "My sister and I have travelled extensively and we want to settle down. We haven't decided precisely where we want to live, but we thought we would rent while we were deciding. Our dear friend here got divorced, and was left penniless, so she moved in with us."

I had no idea Matilda was going to say that and I shifted uncomfortably from one foot to another.

"Oh my goodness! That's dreadful!" Iris said in what was clearly a genuine tone. "It's amazing how many women miss out when they get divorced."

I thought I might as well play along. After all, I couldn't be any more embarrassed than I was now. "I'd signed a pre-nup entirely in his favor," I told her, "but I didn't ever think we'd divorce. In the back of my mind I thought that even if we did divorce, he'd be fair to me, but he wasn't."

Iris nodded slowly. "You'd be surprised how many women I've heard that from."

"I don't believe in divorce," I added.

"And yet you're still divorced," she said. "It only takes one."

I smiled ruefully. "He ran off with a woman a fraction of his age and now they have a baby."

"And he broke the news to Jane on her fiftieth birthday," Matilda added with relish.

Iris reached forward and patted my arm ever so briefly. "If you marry again, make sure you get a very good lawyer first. That's my advice."

I nodded.

"Now about your requirements, Miss Birtwistle…"

"Call me Matilda, please."

"Matilda, your requirements for a house are simply three bedrooms, two bathrooms, and a safe area for a cat. Is that correct?"

"And an area for a garden," Matilda added.

I wondered why Matilda had given genuine requirements as if she were really looking for a house, but I heard someone say once that good liars are those who stick closest to the truth.

The first house Iris showed us looked wildly out of budget—not that we had a budget, but if we did, it would not have stretched to this house. I wondered what Matilda told her our budget was. I figured she had named a rather exorbitant price to have Iris more eager to help us.

Matilda and Eleanor sailed into the living room.

"This is a former Amish house," Iris told us. "It comes with five acres so it has plenty of room for your cat to roam around safely and as you can see, it has an established garden as well as apple trees."

"What happened to the previous owners?" I asked her.

"An elderly gentleman who has gone to stay with his children," Iris said.

I nodded. That was the Amish way.

She opened the door and we walked in. There was no furniture and the place looked plain. It was a typical, simple Amish house.

"Is there electricity?" I asked her.

Iris looked put out. "Well no, but it wouldn't take much to connect. All you have to do is fix a few fences, connect the electricity, and do some things like that. That's why it's such a good low price, a true bargain in fact. There is a gas powered washing machine in the basement."

Both Eleanor and Matilda pulled a face. "That will be the first thing to go," Matilda said. "We actually do want a house with electricity. We don't want to bother ourselves having to worry about things like that."

Iris did not appear concerned by the negative remark. "Have a look around, ladies. Discuss it amongst yourselves and then come back here and tell me what you think." She ushered us up the stairs.

The house reminded me of my childhood. I wanted to speak with Matilda and Eleanor but I figured our voices would carry. After all, there was no hum of electricity through the house. We carried on through the house and walked back down the stairs. "So no internet and no phone lines," I said.

"Everyone has cell phones these days," Iris said with a dismissive wave of her hand. "This house is under your budget, so there's plenty of money left over to have this house fixed the way you would like it."

"Mr. Crumbles would enjoy the fields," I said.

"Who's Mr. Crumbles?" Iris asked me.

"Matilda and Eleanor's cat," I said.

"And there's plenty of room to grow our herbs," Eleanor said. "In fact, there seem to be plenty of herbs here already. I don't think we should rule it out."

"I don't like it as much as you two do," Matilda said, pulling a face of distaste.

If I hadn't known better, I would have thought the sisters were genuine buyers.

"The next house is on the edge of town," Iris

said. "It was part of the Bed and Breakfast. The land is on two titles. The Bed and Breakfast people are selling their business, so they are selling this parcel of land with the house separately."

"How much land is there with this one?" Matilda asked her.

"An acre with this one," she said. "There's a lovely little creek forming the boundary at the back."

This house was quite pretty. It was painted white and the gray roof set it off nicely.

"This house has electricity and internet," Matilda said, rubbing her hands.

After we looked around the house, Iris tried the hard sell. "You seem to like this house, ladies?"

We all nodded and Matilda said, "Oh yes, I really do like this house with the lovely little creek with ducks. In fact, the whole area is lovely."

"What would it take for you to make an offer?" Iris said.

"We just have to decide whether we want to buy that house on the Greek island or live here," Matilda said. "You see, we wanted to live in the apartment a few more months, but now we have to move out in a hurry and we don't want to go back to Greece quite yet, do we, Eleanor?"

Eleanor shook her head. "Oh, no, no, no. Not yet."

"Quite so." Matilda nodded at me. "And as our friend Jane here doesn't want to move to Greece with us this point, it has really pushed our hand in thinking we should buy a house here instead of buying a house in Greece."

My head was reeling from the convoluted explanation, but Iris appeared to be hanging on every word.

Matilda pushed on. "We feel we have to move out of the apartment in a hurry, because it's above a cupcake store and a man died in there recently."

A glimmer of what I took for recognition flashed across Iris's face.

"It was awful," I said. "The poor man collapsed in the store, and he died just after the paramedics took him away."

"Jane was there at the time," Matilda said. "Weren't you, Jane?"

"Yes I was, and it was awful," I said honestly.

"So you can see, we don't want to stay in an apartment where a man has died," Matilda said. "It's most distressing."

Apparently we had Iris's interest. "Was it a heart attack?" she asked.

"Oh no. Awful business. He was murdered."

She looked at me and her mouth fell open. "Murdered?"

"Poisoned," I said.

"Yes, awful business," Matilda repeated. "Even more reason why we want to leave the apartment and find somewhere as soon as possible. This house seems to be ideal. We would be hard pressed to find a better one. What do you think, Eleanor?"

"Quite so, quite so."

I wondered if Eleanor had been ordered to agree with everything Matilda said because she certainly wasn't offering much.

Matilda retrieved her phone from her purse, flipped through it and then held it in front of Iris. "That's where we were thinking of settling down on that Greek island," she said. "It's one of our favorite places in the world." After she held the phone under Iris's nose for a few moments she showed it to me. Matilda and Eleanor were on a beach. The water was deep blue. The photo had surely been taken in Greece.

"It's beautiful," Iris said. To me, she said, "It must have been awful for you, finding a body."

"I'm afraid to say the poor man was alive at the time. He collapsed right in front of me," I said. I could see Iris wanted to ask more, so I added, "I thought he was having a heart attack, but I couldn't find any medication on him. The paramedics came quite quickly."

"Yes, the police questioned us all," Matilda said, "but then they found out the poison was administered to him fifteen minutes before he entered the store. By the way, the store is owned by Jane's sister."

"But isn't she Amish?" Iris said, and then looked discomforted.

"How did you know that?" I asked her.

Iris hesitated for a moment before answering. "Oh, it's all over town that the wealthy businessman Colin Greaves died in a cupcake store owned by an Amish woman."

I wondered how she had found out. As far as I knew, it had not been on the news, but maybe the police had told her when they were questioning her, although why they would tell her Rebecca was Amish, I had no idea. After a moment or two, I realized that the detectives had probably told her the name of the cupcake store and she might have driven past and looked in, or even googled it.

"I suppose a very wealthy man like that would have a lot of enemies," I said. "The police said he was administered the poison at least fifteen minutes before he entered the store. There must have been someone in the car with him."

"It was probably his wife," Iris spat.

"What makes you think that?" Matilda asked her.

"Isn't it always the wife?" Iris asked.

Matilda shrugged. "As Jane said, a wealthy man would have a lot of enemies."

"He was trying to buy the building from my sister," I told Iris. "He was going to do a big development. Maybe he had partners in the development and they wanted him out of the way for some reason."

Iris shook her head. "If you ask me, it was his wife." Her eyes glistened with malice. She abruptly changed the subject. "Well, enough of this sad talk. Let's move onto the next house. I'm sure you'll like it. It's a fixer upper to be sure, but it's a good price and you'll have plenty of money left in the budget to do all the repairs."

"What exactly is wrong with it?" Matilda asked her.

"Nothing too serious," Iris said hesitantly. "It will be good after the bathrooms are replaced and maybe even the kitchen. And the roof leaks, but that will soon be fixed when the roof is replaced. It can be done well within your budget. You will have money left over."

As Iris drove us to the next house, I thought things over. She had a genuine dislike of Stephanie Greaves, but that was to be understood. I didn't get the feeling that she had murdered Greaves, as her venom had seemed directed at his wife rather than at him, but then again who would know? I was certainly no expert on these matters. I was anxious to hear Matilda's opinion.

CHAPTER 16

Since I had returned home and was living in my sister, Rebecca's apartment, I had attended a small church not far from the apartment. It wasn't such a warm and welcoming church, but I enjoyed the sermons. I tended to keep to myself anyway as I didn't want to answer the inevitable questions and end up telling everyone that my husband had run off with a younger woman, had a baby, and divorced me.

I had intended to look around for another church, but I was comfortable enough where I was, so it hadn't really mattered. The church I was sitting in now was huge and opulent, more like a cathedral than a church. At least it was so big that Eleanor, Matilda, and I wouldn't be noticed.

Members of the press were in attendance as was a television crew, and I had caught sight of Detective McCloud and Detective Stirling from a distance.

Matilda leaned over to me and whispered, "Detectives always attend a funeral because the murderers always attend."

"Why do the murderers attend?" I asked, puzzled. "Isn't it a bit of a dead giveaway if they do, no pun intended?"

Matilda chuckled. "I'm not a psychologist. I'm just an amateur sleuth. I don't know why they attend, but they do. It's a well-known fact."

I frowned. "Well that may be so, but it's a little unsettling to think we might be in the same church as the murderer."

"Or murderers," Matilda said. "Maybe two people were in it together. I keep saying this, but no one seems to be listening."

I looked down at the funeral program. "This is quite ornate especially since it was done in such a hurry."

"Clearly, money has been spent," Matilda said. "Obviously Stephanie did it to cover her tracks."

Once more I was puzzled. "Why would she do that?"

"Well, if she gave the vic a generic funeral and

kept the cost low, that would make the police suspicious."

"I suppose so." By now I had learned it was better for me to agree with Matilda. It was easier that way. "There are so many people here, Matilda. What do you think we can gain from attending?"

Matilda shrugged. "I have no idea, but the police wouldn't be here if they thought there was nothing to gain, would they?"

I had to admit she was right. "That makes sense, I suppose. Still, I don't know what we can find out. The murderer is hardly likely to jump to his or her feet and confess. I would think the murderer would be on their very best behavior and try to keep a low profile."

Matilda tapped her chin. "Perhaps, but you can never really be sure, can you?" With that she elbowed me in the ribs. "Shush, it's about to begin."

I looked over at her and Eleanor. They were both staring at the minister. Eleanor was now wearing bright pink rollers that matched her bright pink dress. I was still wondering why she never took them out, and now they were even color-coordinated.

The minister signaled to the choir and everyone sang the first hymn, *Amazing Grace*.

I cried, as I always did when I heard Amazing Grace. I saw Matilda and Eleanor looking at me with puzzlement. When the hymn ended, everyone sat down. The minister then read Psalm 25.

When the minister came to an end, he nodded to someone on the front row. It was too far away for me to see, but a young man stood up and walked to the pulpit.

It was Brooks.

Matilda leaned over. "He's in it with his mother for sure," she hissed. "The two of them stand to inherit."

"His own father?" I whispered back. "Why?"

"I just told you! To get the money, of course."

I sighed. "Yes, I know that," I said slowly, "but he couldn't have had a good relationship with his father, could he? I mean if he was going to murder him. They must've been at loggerheads."

"I don't know. He might have been a spoiled rich kid and his father didn't give him everything he wanted," Matilda said. "And today he's wearing all black to match his mother."

"It *is* a funeral," I pointed out. "Most people here are wearing black, all except for that lady down there near the front."

Matilda half rose before sitting back down abruptly. "Isn't that Iris Ogilvie?"

I craned my neck. "It's hard to tell from behind, but it could be. She *is* wearing rainbow colors. Would that be her husband Richard next to her?"

"How could I possibly know that from here?" Matilda said. "I'll have to find out afterwards. And why on earth is the vic's mistress going to his funeral?"

"Perhaps she was in love with him," I pointed out.

"Yes, but she would want to keep a low profile, wouldn't she? And Stephanie already knows about her. This could get interesting."

"But she doesn't know that Stephanie knows," I said. "But you're right—what excuse would Iris give her husband to get him to attend the funeral? She can hardly tell her husband that her lover was murdered and so she would like to attend his funeral."

Eleanor leaned across Matilda and said in low tones, "Obviously either Richard or Iris Ogilvie or maybe both knew the vic in another capacity—I mean a capacity other than Iris being his mistress."

It all made sense. "True. He might be a business partner or something," I offered.

I looked up and noticed Brooks had already finished speaking. I wished I had listened to what he had said because it might have given me an inkling as to his relationship with his father. Then again, he would hardly be likely to tell it like it was. He would of course avoid all his father's bad points and present him in a favorable light.

Stephanie was the next to stand to speak. She spoke in icy cold tones about what a wonderful person her husband was.

"She's not coming across as believable at all," Matilda said.

The woman in front turned around and looked at Matilda. I thought she was going to berate her, but she smiled and nodded before turning back. It seemed we were not the only ones to have that opinion.

"We'll have to speak with Iris later," Matilda continued.

"Won't she be embarrassed that she hadn't told us that she knew Colin Greaves?" I asked her.

"That's her problem," Matilda retorted. "If it puts her on the spot, then all the better. I also think we need to keep an eye on the people the police are watching."

"Maybe they're keeping an eye on me," I said. My spirits sank.

"I noticed Detective McCloud looking over at you," Eleanor said. "He was certainly watching you."

"Maybe he has a crush on Jane," Matilda said. "I've been watching both detectives and Stirling hasn't looked this way once."

Thankfully, another hymn saved me from the awkward response that was running through my mind.

Stephanie had finished speaking. She dabbed at her eyes in a perfunctory fashion with a tissue and then sat down. I would have thought a murderer would put a little more effort into pretending to be upset. I looked with great interest for other people to speak about Greaves.

Five more people spoke, all men, and all had been business partners of Greaves. They painted him in a wonderful light saying he was a man who would do anything for a friend. I really doubted it was true.

After a final hymn, the minister thanked everyone for coming and said refreshments would be served in a side room. He nodded to his left.

"This will give us a better opportunity to grill

the suspects," Matilda said. She jumped to her feet in a quick and nimble manner and was halfway to the door before I had even stood up. I wondered where she got all her energy. I wasn't much more than half her age and I was already tired solely from being a suspect. The stress was exhausting.

Eleanor and I walked into the room and I spotted Matilda standing near a large urn. "Coffee, I hope," Eleanor said.

We hurried over to Matilda. She had already poured three cups of coffee. It smelled horribly bitter, so I spooned in some extra sugar. I took a sip. It wasn't as bad as it looked. In fact, it tasted bearable, if not nice. I was about to comment on that fact when Eleanor waved in an animated fashion. "Iris! Iris!" she called to her across the room.

Iris Ogilvie hurried over to us. "You didn't tell us you knew the victim," Matilda said with a wide smile. She had managed to keep any note of accusation from her tone.

"My husband knows him. I don't know him at all," Iris said in what was clearly a blatant lie. I knew she knew him and only too well.

I spoke up. "Oh, was your husband a business partner of Mr. Greaves?"

Iris shook her head. "No, Richard owns a law firm. Mr. Greaves was a client of my husband's."

"Oh, a lawyer. I see," I said.

Perhaps Iris thought she had been protesting too much because she added, "Ah, well, I had met Mr. Greaves once or twice when he had dinner with my husband."

"Oh, and his wife?" I said. It was my not-so-subtle way of finding out whether she had met Stephanie. Stephanie had given no inkling that she knew Iris in person.

"No, not Stephanie," Iris said. "Richard and I used to live in New York, and we had dinner with Mr. Greaves once or twice when he was visiting New York."

So that's how they met, I thought. *And Stephanie hadn't met Iris. That makes sense.*

I looked up to see Detective McCloud looking at me. As soon as I caught his eye, he looked away. *Does he really suspect me?* I wondered. *Now he's watching me speak with Iris. What if he thinks Iris and I were in it together?*

I also wondered why Iris hadn't mentioned to us the previous day that she knew Colin Greaves. Maybe it was entirely innocent, after all. Why should she tell a bunch of strangers any details of her personal life?

I wondered how I could investigate Richard Ogilvie. I certainly didn't have enough money to go to his office and pretend to be a client to fish for information. We had already spoken with Stephanie and Iris. Now we need to speak with Iris's husband, Richard. But how? I simply couldn't think of a single ploy. Maybe Matilda would come up with something.

Iris was chatting to Matilda when I took my leave and went in search of cookies. I looked around at what was on offer. It brought me back to my time in the Amish, when we had a lovely time of fellowship after the church services, or meetings as the Amish in my community called them. They happened every other Sunday and afterwards everyone had a lot to eat, the men and the women and the children all eating separately.

My favorite food then had been what the Amish called *church spread*, a mixture of peanut butter, marshmallows, maple syrup, butter, and corn syrup. Although it had been my favorite, I hadn't eaten it once in all those years since I had left the Amish.

"Miss Delight."

I nearly dropped my cookie, and spun around.

It was Detective McCloud. "What are you doing here?" he said.

"I could ask you the same thing." It was a silly thing to say, but it was the first thing that came to my head.

He looked as though he was trying to suppress a smile. "I'm a detective and we always attend the funerals of victims," he said.

I nodded. "That's what Matilda said."

"You haven't answered my question."

I bit back the urge to say something sarcastic, and instead said, "I came here because I wanted to pay my respects. After all, I was there when he collapsed and I tried to help him although it was unsuccessful." And that was the truth—even if I hadn't been a murder suspect, I would still have attended Colin Greaves's funeral.

"I see. And how do you know Iris Ogilvie?"

I had to think quickly. "Eleanor and Matilda are thinking about buying a house," I said. "Iris is a realtor. Why would you ask?" I plastered an innocent look on my face. Detective McCloud had no way of knowing I knew that Iris Ogilvie had been Colin Greaves's mistress.

"We were surprised to see her here," I said, and that also was true. "She told us her husband

195

was Mr. Greaves's lawyer. It's a small world, isn't it!"

Detective McCloud took a step closer to me and I took a step back instinctively. "Miss Delight, have a look around the room now and tell me if you can see the person who has been following you."

I did as he asked, and at the same time, I said, "But I have never seen his face."

"No, but I'm sure you have good instincts, Jane. You have seen his outline and the way he moves, and I'd like you to keep an eye out for him. Even if you aren't sure and only have a small suspicion, I'd still rather you voice it to me. Do we have a deal?"

"Sure." I had to admit, the fact that he had praised my instincts made me flush warm from the tip of my head right down to my toes.

CHAPTER 17

*R*ebecca and I were cleaning the store after the close of business for the day and Eleanor and Matilda were helping us.

Presently, Eleanor looked up from her mop. "I've been thinking about it ever since the funeral, and I can't think of a way we can investigate Richard Ogilvie."

I agreed. "Yes, he *is* an expensive lawyer, so none of us can pretend we have a legal problem because we don't have the money to pay the fees."

"He probably plays golf," Eleanor said. "One of us could pretend to play golf."

Matilda sighed dramatically. "Oh Eleanor, that won't work. It won't work at all."

Eleanor was visibly put out. "Why not?"

Matilda shook her head. "It just doesn't work like that. See, I have no idea what we could do."

"We don't have to speak to him in person," I said. "Maybe we could google him and find out something about him."

"I googled him on my phone while you two were drinking coffee and eating cookies after the funeral," Eleanor told us. "It doesn't help at all. I mean I found a lot about the man but nothing that would give us any clues as to why he or his wife would want to murder Colin Greaves."

"It's obvious why his wife wanted to," Matilda said. "She wanted him for herself, and he refused to leave Stephanie for her."

"That's pure speculation," I said. "Richard was Greaves's lawyer, so he would have known his secrets. But I can't see how that helps us."

Rebecca finally spoke for the first time in the conversation. "If he did murder Mr. Greaves, then it was probably a business deal gone wrong."

I scratched my head. "How do we find out about that?"

Rebecca stopped wiping down the countertop and looked up at me. "Isn't it obvious?"

"If it was obvious I would have thought of it by now," I said dryly.

"Your ex-husband is a lawyer."

At first I wondered what she meant and then it dawned on me. "No, no, no," I stammered. "No way!"

It seemed Matilda and Eleanor had already caught on. "Why, that's perfect! You can ask your ex-husband." Matilda rubbed her hands with glee.

"I don't want to speak to him," I protested. "We haven't spoken to each other since the divorce."

"You have nothing to be ashamed about," Eleanor said. "What do you have to lose by calling him?"

"Only my sanity," I muttered. "Anyway, how would I explain the reason I wanted to know? I can hardly tell him that I'm a suspect in a murder case and so I'm investigating all of the other suspects, one of whom is the hotshot lawyer Richard Ogilvie."

"That's exactly what you're going to tell him," Matilda said in an encouraging tone. "Call him now and get it over with. It will be like ripping off a Band-Aid."

"What if Cherri answers the phone?" I said with a shudder.

"Then just ask to speak to what's-his-name," Eleanor said.

"Ted," I supplied.

"You could always hang up and call again later," Matilda said. "It's entirely up to you, but the only way we can find out about Richard Ogilvie is to ask your ex-husband."

"Okay, okay, I'll do it," I said and then added, "but it's against my better judgment."

I had left my phone in the kitchen so I went back to fetch it. "Do you want us all to leave?" Matilda asked me.

"No, I need you all here for backup," I said. I took a deep breath and punched the buttons. It went straight to voicemail. I left a message for Ted to call me back.

"Well, you all heard that," I said. "He'll have to call me back."

"What if he doesn't?" Matilda said. "He probably feels the same way about you that you feel about him. In that case, he won't call you back. He'll probably be annoyed that you called him too. He will probably think you're after money."

"Thanks for such encouraging words," I said sarcastically. Just then my phone rang. I looked down at the caller ID. "It's him!" I hissed. My blood ran cold.

My mouth was dry and I was worried I'd have a fit of coughing. "Hello, Jane speaking."

"What do you want?" was the curt reply.

"I want to ask you a question about another lawyer."

"Are you thinking about taking legal action against me?" asked Ted.

I hurried to reassure him. "No, no." I took a deep breath and launched into my explanation. "A man died in Rebecca's store and the police said he had been poisoned. The victim was having an affair with the wife of someone you might know, Richard Ogilvie."

I heard a sharp intake of breath and then a young female voice calling out in the background, "Who is it, Popsicle?"

"Popsicle?" I repeated, and at once regretted saying it. I quickly added, "Do you know Richard Ogilvie?"

"Everyone knows Richard Ogilvie," Ted said.

"Well, I don't know him," I pointed out.

Ted snorted rudely. "I mean anyone important, you know, like a lawyer. The lawyers all know him."

"So he's some sort of commercial lawyer, I take it?"

"Yes. His currency is in secrets. His clients are

mostly millionaires and some would say his clients are those with shady dealings."

My phone was on speaker and I looked up to see Matilda nodding.

"This might sound strange, Ted, but do you think Richard could have possibly murdered Colin Greaves if he found out his wife was having an affair with Greaves?"

"Don't be ridiculous," my husband snapped. "You've been watching too much TV, Jane."

Matilda snatched the phone from me. "Mr. Delight? This is Matilda Birtwistle. I'm investigating this case and I'd like to ask you some questions about Richard Ogilvie. Do you think he had illicit business dealings with Colin Greaves? Off the record, of course."

The phone was still on speaker so I heard Ted say, "I have no idea, no idea at all. Why don't you go and ask Richard?"

I snatched the phone back. "That's a good one, Ted. Are you suggesting we ask Richard Ogilvie if he murdered Colin Greaves because his wife was having an affair with him? And what if he doesn't know his wife was having an affair?"

"Then he wouldn't have a motive, now would he?"

I winced at my husband's sarcastic voice. Still, I needed to find out more information. "Well then, Ted, is there anything else you can tell us about Richard Ogilvie or his law firm? Anything at all?"

The line went silent for what seemed an age. I thought Ted had hung up. After a lengthy interval, he spoke. "You didn't hear this from me, but Richard doesn't have the best of reputations. Not amongst the other lawyers, that is. I heard some things from time to time that suggested he wasn't completely on the level. I can't be certain, mind you. It's all hearsay and innuendo. It might have been simply jealousy, but I heard it from more than one source."

"Do you think he could be capable of murder?"

"I sincerely doubt it," my ex-husband said. "However, Richard would have known all his clients' dirty little secrets, but that would have only given the clients the motive to murder him, not the other way around. Now is that all, Jane? I'm a very busy man." With that, he hung up.

I stared at the phone for some time. I could almost feel the steam coming out of my ears. "Why you, you…" I sputtered.

"I wouldn't finish that sentence if I were you," Matilda said, pointing to my sister. "There's an

Amish person present who wouldn't have heard such language before."

"I wasn't going to call him anything like that," I protested. "Anyway, can you believe the nerve of him? I wish there was some other way to find out more about Richard Ogilvie."

"I'd like to set Richard on the back burner for now," Matilda said. "He is a possibility, although not a strong one. So far, Stephanie, her son, and Richard's wife are the main suspects. Hmm, although there is always the possibility that Richard and Iris were in it together."

"I always come back to the fact that someone was probably in the car with him when they administered the fatal dose," I said. "We need to find out where Richard was on that day and whether he had an alibi. In fact, we need to find out if all our suspects had alibis."

Matilda snapped her fingers. "I know! Let's see if Richard Ogilvie was in court that day."

"Genius!" I exclaimed, just as a streak flashed through my legs.

"Mr. Crumbles!" Matilda said.

"How did you get down here?" Rebecca said, clearly concerned. "What if the Health Department sees him?"

"I only had the door between the apartment and the store open a tiny little bit," Matilda said. "He must have opened it with his little paw. Isn't he so clever!"

The look on Rebecca's face showed she did not agree.

A loud knock on the store door startled us all. I looked up. It was Detective McCloud, and his expression was grim.

CHAPTER 18

"Miss Delight, I'm going to have to ask you to come downtown with me. We have some questions."

I went cold all over. Surely they wouldn't arrest me?

"I'll just get my purse," I said.

"We'll pray for you," Rebecca called after my departing back.

Detective Stirling was waiting outside, leaning back against the police vehicle and looking quite bored. He opened the back door for me. Thankfully he didn't put his hand on my head like they do on those TV shows, and I hadn't been arrested yet, but that was small comfort to me.

"Am I under arrest?" I said to both detectives from the back seat of the vehicle.

"We were hoping you could clear up a couple of things for us," Detective McCloud said.

It sounded all the more ominous. I had no idea what was going on. I had no choice but to comply.

This time they parked the car around the back of the building and I was led through the back door down a labyrinth of corridors and into an interview room. This one was not like the interview room I had been in before and it did have a large mirror on one wall, which I realized was a two-way mirror. I wondered if anyone was looking through it at me right at this minute. I resisted the bizarre desire to wave.

McCloud left, and was replaced by a thin, younger detective by the name of Sykes.

The preliminaries went through in a blur. Detective Stirling asked me my name, age, and address, which I had already given them, but I wasn't going to point that out.

"Can I get you anything?" Stirling asked. "Coffee, water?"

I shook my head. "No thanks."

"Would you tell us your movements for the day

of Colin Greaves's murder?" This time it was Detective Sykes who spoke.

"Well, I woke up as usual in my apartment, and then I hurried around cleaning the apartment because Matilda and Eleanor were arriving that day. Then I went down to work in my sister's store as I always do."

"How long was Greaves in the store?" Detective Stirling asked me.

"About five minutes."

"Are you sure?"

I nodded. "Yes."

"Did you leave the store at any point through the day before Greaves's visit?"

"No."

Stirling gave me a half nod. "Please think about it before you answer, Miss Delight," he said. "This is important, so take as long as you need to remember."

"I don't need time to remember," I said. "I didn't go anywhere. I just woke up, cleaned the apartment, walked down the stairs to the store, and worked in the store. I didn't go outside at all."

Sykes looked up from his paperwork. "You didn't go outside once?"

"That's correct," I said.

"You didn't go to a café?" Stirling said. "You didn't run any errands?"

I shifted in my seat. This room had a stale smell, as though it hadn't been used in a while, but it was spotlessly clean. "No. I've already told you I didn't leave at all."

"You haven't mentioned eating breakfast, having coffee anything like that."

I haven't mentioned cleaning my teeth either, I silently added. Aloud, I said, "Obviously, I had coffee, but it was in my apartment. Rebecca and I had coffee together in the back room of the store, but I can assure you I did not leave the building at all that day until the time Mr. Greaves collapsed."

"Did any of your friends enter the shop that day?" Stirling asked me.

"I don't have any friends," I said and then winced when Sykes shot me a strange look. I decided to explain. "I don't really know anyone in town apart from my sister and her family. I go to church on Sundays, but I haven't really met anyone there. I only know people to say hello to and I haven't really made any friends here."

Stirling leaned back in his seat, his arms locked behind his head. He put his arms behind his neck, his fingers interlocked. "Do you expect me to believe that you have been here six months and you haven't made any friends at all? Not a single friend?"

I bristled. "That's none of your business," I said. "Surely it is not a crime not to make friends!" I crossed my arms over my chest and glared at him.

Stirling appeared unperturbed. "And you allege you hadn't met the Birtwistle sisters either?"

"I don't allege anything," I said. "It's the truth. I had never met them before they came into Rebecca's store that afternoon."

"Had you ever spoken with them on the phone prior to that day?"

I shook my head. "No, but we've already been over this. How many times do I have to go over and over this?"

Stirling landed his chair with a thud. "Until we are completely satisfied, Miss Delight. So are you saying you had never spoken with Matilda or Eleanor Birtwistle until they arrived in the store that day?"

"That's exactly right," I said, more firmly than I intended.

"And what did you have for breakfast?" he asked me.

I was surprised by the question. I mean, what

possible relevance did it have for the case? Still, I did my best to answer. "I had a few cups of coffee for breakfast," I told him. "After we opened the store, there was a lull in customers so Jane and I had coffee and some graham cracker pudding."

Stirling raised his eyebrows. "You said you had several cups of coffee in your apartment? Then you had more soon after? Isn't that a little excessive?"

"Is that illegal?" I said crossly.

"And you didn't eat anything else?"

I had no idea where he was going with this line of questioning. "No I didn't, apart from the graham cracker pudding. You can ask Rebecca."

"Yes, we will do just that," Stirling said. "And your sister can vouch for your whereabouts all that morning?"

"Of course she can. Look, what's all this about?"

"We're just trying to clear some things up," Stirling said after glancing at his partner. He stood up. "That will be all for now, Miss Delight, but please make yourself available for questioning. I'm sure we will want to speak with you again."

"Sure," I said. I felt like some sort of criminal. It quite unnerved me.

"We will have a uniformed officer take you

home," Stirling said. The two detectives left the room, although I was sure the other detective shot me an apologetic look.

Two uniformed officers entered the room shortly afterwards and said they'd give me a ride home. They were quite nice and chatty and so by the time I arrived home, I felt a little more comfortable and at ease.

My mood changed as soon as I entered the apartment.

"Detective McCloud was here questioning us," Matilda blurted out.

"What about?" I asked her.

"He was going on and on asking us whether we had ever met you before, and he also questioned Rebecca downstairs in her shop."

I was horrified. "What about?" I said again.

"The same sort of thing," Matilda said. "Rebecca said they were asking her if you had ever spoken with us on the phone or whether you knew us before. They also looked through our fridge and took photos, and they looked through our trash. They also asked what you normally eat for breakfast."

"And they asked Rebecca how long the vic was

in her store. They also asked her what you'd eaten that day before the vic died," Matilda chimed in.

"I have no idea what this is all about." I sat on the chair and narrowly avoiding sitting on the little cat. "I'm so sorry, Mr. Crumbles," I said. He shot me a disdainful look.

"What are we going to do?" I asked Matilda and Eleanor. "They obviously think it was me."

Matilda shook a finger at me. "No, it's just that the alibis of the other suspects must have all checked out. They're probably just doing the rounds again starting with you."

I threw my hands in the air. "But then who could it be?" I checked the suspects off one by one on my fingers. "Stephanie Greaves, her son, Brooks, Iris Ogilvie, Richard Ogilvie, William and Mia Willow."

"Maybe there is someone we don't know about," Eleanor said. "Maybe it's someone the police don't know about either."

I slumped forward, my head in my hands. "That's no comfort to me, I'm afraid."

"Never you mind," Matilda said. "I've put two and two together, and I've asked Rebecca to stop by to see someone on her way home."

Now I really was intrigued. "Do go on."

"Well, it's like this. The police were awfully interested in the food. What does that tell you?"

"Not a thing to be honest," I said, silently berating myself for having minimal sleuthing skills.

"The medical examiner has obviously given the police the report of the contents of the vic's stomach," Matilda said. "We know that the perpetrator poisoned the vic, and we assume the poison was administered orally. If so, it had to be concealed in food. They wanted to know what you had eaten that day. Therefore, they were wondering whether you shared it with Mr. Greaves."

I was horrified. "You mean the police were wondering if I had eaten the same type of food that was found in Greaves's stomach?"

Matilda jabbed her finger in the air. "Exactly! You finally caught on, Jane. That's good. And Rebecca has gone to speak with Wanda Hershberger and she is going to ask her daughter to find out exactly what that food was. We will go there tomorrow and I'll find out more from Mrs. Hershberger. Isn't that great!"

Matilda was quite excited, but I didn't share her happiness. Still, I didn't want to disappoint her, so I smiled and nodded. How would it help us to know what food the victim had ingested?

CHAPTER 19

*M*atilda, Eleanor, and I arrived at Wanda Hershberger's *grossmammi haus*. This time, I had insisted upon driving, although Matilda was quite eager to do so. My nerves were already frayed.

Wanda met us at the door with a wide smile. "Come in, all of you. I've been expecting you. Of course you'll stay for lunch."

I thought Eleanor and Matilda might protest so I shook my head at them as we walked behind Wanda in the direction of her kitchen. It was commonplace for visitors to arrive unannounced in the Amish community at mealtimes and they were always fed.

"I was preparing pot pie," Wanda said.

"What can I do to help?" I asked her. She immediately assigned me to roll out the dough for the noodles. I knew the strips would dry on the back of a chair before being cut into rectangles. Matilda and Eleanor also offered to help so they were assigned the stew.

"Did you find out anything from your daughter?" I asked Wanda.

"Yes, quite a bit," she said. "She said a fatal dose of aconitine is quite tiny, from one to six and half milligrams, but she also said that there are different types of wolfsbane and giving the actual plant itself would obviously require much higher doses than giving the actual drug."

"Interesting," I said, but I also didn't see how that would help.

Wanda was still talking. "She said he took the poison orally."

"You mean he wasn't injected?" I asked.

She nodded. "Yes, apparently in some cultures in historical times, people put wolfsbane on the tips of their arrows. The plants are quite poisonous to touch and can be absorbed through the skin, but if absorbed through the skin, there will be no gastrointestinal effects and there were with the man in question."

"That makes sense," I said. "He was given a fatal oral dose."

"Yes, my daughter said it was definitely in something he ate."

"Did your daughter happen to mention the contents of his stomach?" Matilda asked her.

Wanda looked up from sprinkling some ground turmeric into the stew. "Yes, potatoes, chicken, cheese, bacon, tomato, onion and garlic, and truffle. All were in very small amounts."

"Truffle?" I said in surprise.

"Yes, and chocolate cake and frosting," she said.

Matilda pulled a face. "It doesn't sound a nice combination. At least that explains why the police asked Rebecca if she ever sold savory cupcakes."

"She never has," I said, "so it looks like the murderer fed Colin Greaves something savory."

"My daughter found out that wolfsbane has a slightly bitter taste," Wanda added, "but it's only slightly bitter. She said a fatal dose could cause symptoms as soon as fifteen minutes after ingestion."

We all nodded. "Yes, Sarah Beiler told us that."

"And my daughter said severe symptoms could occur as late as two hours after ingestion."

"Well, there's your window," Matilda said.

"Was there severe vomiting?" Wanda asked us.

"Not that I saw," I said.

"That narrows it down even more," Wanda said. "There would be severe vomiting after an hour."

"So that narrows the window down even more in that case," Matilda said.

"Mrs. Hershberger just said that," Eleanor said.

Matilda glared at her.

Wanda did not appear to notice their bickering. "The warm feeling in the mouth and tingling of the tongue happen almost straight away and usually within ten minutes. There can be a strange feeling in the mouth and even a feeling of nausea."

"Hmm, I did notice him licking his lips and he did put his hand to his mouth a couple of times," I said.

Wanda set down a wooden spoon. "I almost forgot to mention. My daughter said the poison has definitely tested for certain as wolfsbane. There no doubt now."

We all nodded once more. That was no surprise to any of us.

Wanda pushed on. "There are several varieties of aconitine and they're all poisonous to different degrees. My daughter also found out that wolfsbane can be mistaken for cardiac arrest. It presents with many of the same symptoms. So if the onset is rapid, it was good that the paramedics realized it wasn't a heart attack," Wanda said.

I took a few moments to process the information. "That's interesting, so perhaps the murderer didn't think he or she would be caught."

"I'll just fetch you a note my daughter wrote." Wanda left the room and returned with a piece of paper covered in handwriting. I read it aloud.

Aconitine alkaloids contain neurotoxins and cardio toxins. Patients predominantly present with gastrointestinal, cardiovascular, and neurological features.

Under that she had written *ventricular arrhythmias* and *cardiogenic shock.*

"There is one thing we can do," I said. "We need to retrace the vic's steps." I scratched my head. I was picking up Matilda's terminology.

"What, how are we going to retrace his steps?" Matilda asked me.

"I don't really know. I suppose I'll have to talk with his wife again."

"I don't think that would go over well," Matilda pointed out, "but I don't have any better ideas."

I thought things through before speaking. "Let's think about it backward. He collapsed in Rebecca's store. He had been touching his mouth which suggests the tingling was already happening, but that happens fairly soon after ingestion of the poison. He didn't have the severe vomiting yet, so it was less than an hour after he had been poisoned. We know he had come from the herbal supplements store directly before that."

"Well, if it wasn't the people who own the health food store, then someone must have been in the car with him," Matilda said, "so it all comes back to the mistress once more. Given the fact Richard Ogilvie is an accomplished lawyer, I don't think he'd have much trouble arranging an alibi for himself or his wife." She tapped her chin. "Still, Richard wouldn't have had any idea that his wife was having an affair with the vic, would he?"

I shrugged. "Will the police tell him now?"

Matilda leaned forward in her chair. "I have no idea."

"Then we're back where we started from," I

said sadly. "Everything is pointing to what we originally thought, that Greaves was administered the fatal dose of poison disguised in food. It must have happened not long before he collapsed in the store. Perhaps we should go and speak with William and Mia Willow from the health food store again and ask them if he mentioned where he had been." I shook my head. "No, that's clutching at straws. Why would he tell them where he had been?"

"I think we're at an impasse," Matilda said. "I simply don't know what else to do."

"And there wouldn't be any witnesses who would possibly remember seeing a random person in a car with the stranger. Surely there must be something we can do to trace Greaves's steps. But who could we ask? Who would know? Did he normally have a driver?"

"Rebecca might know the answer to that," Matilda said. "But did you ever notice a driver?"

I shook my head. "Colin Greaves always came into the store alone and I never saw his car. He was always alone. I don't think Rebecca would know if he had a driver. Who else would?"

"The police would," Eleanor pointed out, "but they are not likely to tell us."

"His wife and his son would know as well, but I really don't feel like asking them again," I said.

Matilda stood up and looked out the window. "We are just going around in circles and we're not getting anywhere. We will have to think of something, because the police are closing in on you, Jane."

I knew she was right. "Okay, I have an idea, but you're not going to like it."

CHAPTER 20

"You were right—I am most certainly not thrilled with your idea," Matilda said.

I sighed. "I'm not exactly thrilled about it either, but the only way we're going to find out if someone was in the car that day is to ask Stephanie."

"She's not going to tell us the truth if she's the murderer or if she's in it with her son, or even if she is covering for her son," Matilda pointed out.

"I know that," I said wearily. "I know this only works if Stephanie isn't the murderer, but it's worth a try. What other choice do we have?"

Matilda was silent for a while and then said, "You're right. We don't have any other leads and it *is* worth a try. After all, what have we got to lose?"

"Our lives possibly, if she is the murderer and comes after us," I said.

Matilda chuckled, but I had been completely serious. "I still think it's a mistake not coming in disguise as your sister," she said.

I shook my head. "Rebecca wouldn't be happy to swap places with me again." *And your driving is quite scary*, I added silently.

Matilda shook her finger at me. "You'll just have to remember to pretend you've never been there before. After all, Stephanie will think she's never met you."

We were close to the tall gates. "I know. I'm really worried that I'll let something slip."

Once more the gates were slightly open and I wondered if they were ever closed. As we approached the large house, a thousand butterflies went crazy in the pit of my stomach. "I don't think this is a good idea after all," I muttered.

"In for a penny, in for a pound," Matilda said brightly. "Let's go!"

She was out of the door and standing on the porch before I had time to gather my wits. I hurried to catch up with her.

Once more Stephanie answered the door. She

was immaculately dressed, as usual. She looked at me with her eyes raised.

"You met my twin sister, Rebecca," I said.

Stephanie's mouth fell open. "You're not Amish!"

"I was once," I said in a hurry to come to the point. "Would you mind if we take a moment of your time? Only a moment, mind you."

Stephanie looked as though she was about to refuse, but ushered us inside. "Celia!" she shrieked. She muttered some rude words under her breath and then said to us, "I don't know why I put up with that woman. She is never here when I want her."

Celia soon appeared. "Fetch drinks for everyone," Stephanie said without telling Celia what drinks to bring.

Celia raised one eyebrow at us. "Strong coffee please," Matilda said.

"I'll have the same, please."

Stephanie took us to the same area where we had been before. I had to keep telling myself to pretend I had not been here before. "You have a beautiful home," I said.

Stephanie simply nodded. "So what can I do for you?"

"I hope my words don't upset you, but I need to be blunt because I'm running out of time. The police questioned my sister Rebecca again last night."

Stephanie interrupted me. "Surely they don't think an Amish woman would do anyone any harm?"

I had been about to add that the police questioned me too, but thought it might be better to stay silent on that point. "Yes, it's quite crazy isn't it," I said. "Anyway, we wanted to know if your husband had a driver."

"Of course he had a driver," Stephanie said, as if it was a crazy question. "Barry Jones. He's been working for my husband for years. Most competent driver."

"Was he driving your husband the day he was poisoned?" I asked her.

Stephanie looked off into the distance. "No, I don't believe he was. Jones suffers from migraines. He gets them on a fairly regular basis."

"What did your husband do when Barry Jones was sick?" I asked her.

Stephanie scoffed at me. "My husband wasn't so precious he couldn't drive himself," she said. "On those days he simply drove himself."

"And he was driving himself the day he was poisoned?"

"Yes, I'm sure of it," Stephanie said.

Matilda spoke for the first time. "And is Barry Jones your driver too?"

Stephanie waved one hand at her and pursed her lips. "Goodness gracious me, no. I prefer to drive myself."

"Does that mean Barry Jones has now left your employ?" I asked her. It was more idle curiosity than anything else.

"Oh no, Jones is now going to drive my son in my husband's car," Stephanie said. "Jones has been with us for years."

Celia returned at that moment and after depositing our coffees on the table, handed Stephanie a cocktail. "Might I ask your interest in my husband's driver?" Stephanie asked. It was more of a demand than a question.

Matilda and I exchanged glances. "Because your husband was poisoned not long before he entered my sister's store," I told her, "so if your husband had a driver that day, we could have asked the driver if he saw anyone give your husband any food."

I thought my words might irritate Stephanie in

some manner, but she simply said, "Yes, your sister did tell me about the timeframe of the poisoning. It would have been a good idea to ask the driver, but Jones wasn't there that day. Jones was sick like I said. The police have already checked that out."

"Your son isn't here today?' Matilda asked her. "Is he at the gym?"

Stephanie's face was a picture of distaste. "Not at all. Poor Brooks simply abhors the gym. His father forced him to go, you see. They didn't get on. In fact, Colin threw Brooks out of the home."

She stood up and smoothed down her clothes with both hands. "Thank you for your visit and your interest in the matter, and I do hope the police don't arrest your sister. It's preposterous to think that an Amish lady would harm anyone, much less murder them."

I thanked her for her time, stood, and turned to go, but Matilda took a large gulp of her coffee and then gasped for air. She waved her hand in front of her mouth. "It's hot," she sputtered.

I hurried out of the house. I couldn't wait to get back in the car and talk it over with Matilda. "What did you think of that?" I asked as we drove away.

"It was such good coffee," she said. "I wish I'd had time to drink it all."

I shook my head. "No, I meant about the case. Interesting she admitted Brooks and Colin had a bad relationship."

Matilda nodded. "And she obviously thought she'd said too much, because she wanted us to leave as soon as she told us that. And she could be making up lies about this Barry person. Maybe he was in the car after all. Maybe he did poison Greaves and maybe Stephanie and Brooks put him up to it."

"But Stephanie did say the police checked the driver out," I said.

Matilda grunted. "A murderer would say that, of course. We can't take her word for it."

"Okay, I'm going to call Detective McCloud." We were driving by a cute little café so I pulled up outside. I motioned for Matilda to be quiet and pulled Detective McCloud's card out of my purse.

To my surprise he answered at once. "Miss Delight, have you seen the prowler again?"

I hurried to reassure him. "No, it's nothing like that. You probably already know this information, but I've just heard that Colin Greaves had a driver by the name of Barry Jones. On the very day Greaves was murdered, Barry Jones had a migraine and wasn't able to drive him."

"Yes, that's correct," Detective McCloud said. "Look, it's kind of you to bring this information to my notice, Miss Delight, but we were already aware of it."

"So it's true?" I pressed him. "Barry Jones really didn't drive the victim that day?"

McCloud hesitated. I wondered if he was considering whether he should tell me to mind my own business. There was such a long interval that I thought he had hung up, but then he said, "Yes, we checked it out and that's correct. Now Miss Delight, how did you come across this information?"

"Hello? Hello?" I said. "You're breaking up. Can you hear me? I'm in my car." With that, I hung up.

Matilda patted me on my back. "You're becoming quite good at this," she said. "Only you're too young for Miss Marple, although *I* am the right age. Good work Jane. So it *is* true—Barry Jones was the vic's driver and he was sick that day."

I had to admit I was quite pleased with myself for finding out the information.

Matilda was still talking. "You know, migraines can be brought on by allergies. What if Stephanie slipped him something to bring on his migraine so he couldn't drive that day, and Brooks went with him and gave him the poison?"

"It's entirely possible, I suppose," I said, "although this is getting awfully convoluted."

"If it wasn't so convoluted, the police would have figured it out by now," Matilda pointed out. "Let's look at the facts. Someone administered the poison to the vic. We know it wasn't in the chocolate cupcake he ate in Rebecca's store, so it must have been in a savory cupcake."

"What makes you think the poison was in a cupcake?" I asked her.

"Because Wanda Hershberger's daughter reported that there was only a small amount of food in the vic's stomach. If he'd had a big meal of bacon, then there would have been more bacon in his stomach. However, it was a small amount which suggests it was something like a savory cupcake, given the fact it was combined with chicken, cheese, and more importantly, truffle. Bacon White Truffle cupcakes are sold at a bakery in this town."

"You really are good at this, Matilda," I said with admiration.

She afforded me a wide smile, and then said, "What shall we do next?" Before I could answer, she added, "I think we should head to William and Mia Willow's store. The vic went there first, and we need to ask them if he was with anyone."

"Good idea," I said, but I couldn't shake the strange feeling that I had missed something.

CHAPTER 21

 hen I got back to Rebecca's store, she said, "You didn't miss anything, Jane. Hardly anyone has been in today. I had one rush of customers, but then nothing since."

"That's a relief," I said. "I didn't like running out on you again."

"You more than make up for it with the baking," Rebecca said. "That's a big load off my mind."

Eleanor came down the stairs. "I thought I heard you there."

"You did lock your cat up, didn't you?" Rebecca said with a quick look at the door.

"Yes, I think he's feeling guilty. He just knocked

something else off the top of the kitchen cupboard."

Matilda made a tut-tutting sound. "I thought we agreed not to put anything up high that could possibly fall since he likes to knock things over!"

Eleanor folded her arms over her chest. "Really, Matilda, how on earth would I know that Mr. Crumbles was going to be able to climb up *that* high! I have no idea how he managed to do it. It's not my fault he's a modern day Houdini."

Matilda rolled her eyes. "Oh really Eleanor, everybody knows Houdini was an escape artist. He didn't climb up on furniture and knock things over."

Eleanor frowned. " Matilda, you pick on everything I say."

Rebecca shot me a look and then said, "So how did your sleuthing go today? Did Stephanie realize you were the same person that she saw last time?"

"She had no idea at all," Matilda told her. "You know, the more I think about it, the murderers are definitely Stephanie and Brooks."

"I don't think they were in it together," I said. "I think it's the son."

"Whatever makes you say that?" Eleanor asked me.

Before I had a chance to answer, Matilda spoke. "Think of it this way. Brooks had a bad relationship with his father. Maybe his father said he wanted nothing more to do with him and Stephanie was afraid he would cut Brooks out of the will. His father just happened to die before he was able to cut Brooks out of the will. What do you think of that?"

"I don't think that really helps us," I said. "If Colin Greaves cut his son out of the will, then he would have left the son's share to the mother, and after Greaves died, Stephanie would have simply given it to her son."

Matilda looked downcast. "Actually, that hadn't occurred to me. You're right. Still, Brooks and his father didn't get on at all well and it's clear that Stephanie wanted Brooks back home."

"But would she actually murder her husband just because he was mean to her son and wouldn't allow him in the house?" Eleanor said. "It seems a bit extreme to me."

"Murder is always extreme," I pointed out. "Besides, that wasn't the only reason Stephanie was upset with her husband. She had a private detective investigating him, and had found out only recently that he was having an affair with Iris Ogilvie."

Matilda shook her head. "You heard her say that her marriage had been over for years."

"That's assuming she told us the truth," I said. "She is hardly going to say she was devastated about the affair because that would give her a motive."

"Let's look at what we do know." Matilda tapped on the countertop for attention, despite the fact we were all listening to her. "It had to be someone who had access to wolfsbane. *We* have access to wolfsbane, but we know it wasn't us. William and Mia Willow have access to wolfsbane. It could have been them. Stephanie and Brooks had access to wolfsbane, and what's more, Stephanie was a Traditional Chinese Medicine practitioner before she met her husband so she would have the knowledge to process the wolfsbane."

"But does it need much processing?" I asked her. "Aren't the leaves and the roots poisonous?"

Eleanor nodded. "Quite so. I think what Matilda means is that Stephanie could have processed it into a really nasty dose."

"You don't need to speak for me," Matilda said. "I myself am quite capable of explaining what I mean."

I spoke quickly to avoid another argument. "As

far as we know, Iris Ogilvie and her husband Richard Ogilvie didn't have access to wolfsbane."

"Yes, that's true," Matilda said. "Do you think we can cross them off our list?"

I nodded. "I do. It's a coincidence that several of us have wolfsbane, but it would be far too much of a coincidence if one or both of the Ogilvies knew the other suspects had access to wolfsbane and actually framed one of us."

Eleanor frowned. "And if they were trying to frame one of us in particular, then they did a very bad job."

"That's the cleverest thing you've said all day, maybe all year," Matilda said to her sister.

Eleanor looked confused. No doubt she was wondering whether it was a compliment or an insult. I know I sure was wondering. I turned to Rebecca.

"If you think I've got time between customers, I'll just pop out and speak with William Willow."

"What do you possibly have to ask him now?" Rebecca said.

"I want to know if he saw anyone with Colin Greaves," I told her. "Maybe Colin Greaves came in with someone."

Matilda interrupted me. "No, of course he

wouldn't have. Whoever poisoned Colin Greaves would have been sure to stay out of sight."

"I'm still asking. You never know," I said.

I half expected Eleanor or Matilda to want to come with me, but Eleanor wanted to wash her hair, no doubt so she could put a fresh batch of rollers in it, and Matilda said it was time for her hot yoga class.

It was a pleasant walk to the health food store owned by the Willows. When I walked in, I didn't see any customers, and William and Mia were clearly arguing. I cleared my throat to alert them to the fact I was there, and then abruptly sneezed when the incense tickled my throat.

They stopped arguing at once and both plastered smiles on their faces. "How are you today, Jane?" Mia asked me.

"I'm a little concerned because the police questioned us all again last evening," I told them.

They both looked shocked. "What, not again?" Mia said.

"They didn't question either of you yesterday?" I said.

They both shook their heads. A customer walked in and immediately asked them a question. Mia took the lady aside to discuss her health issues.

"William, I wanted to ask you if you ever saw anyone with Colin Greaves."

William rubbed his chin. "What do you mean?"

I did not know how to put it any more plainly. "I mean, was he ever accompanied by anyone?"

William shook his head. "No one at all. He was always alone."

"Did you ever see anyone in the car with him?"

"I never saw his car," William said. "He always came in here alone."

Another dead end, I thought. Aloud, I said, "Did you know he had a driver?"

"Oh yes, I knew that," William said. "The man had terrible migraines."

It was my turn to be surprised. "How did you know that?"

William looked up from rearranging bottles. "Mr. Greaves told me of course. We always discussed his driver's migraines. Mr. Greaves occasionally bought Sheng Jiang, Bai Shao, and Gan Cao for his driver."

"I didn't realize Colin Greaves was into alternate medicine or herbal remedies."

"Oh yes. He said his wife was a Traditional Chinese Medicine practitioner and that's how they met. He was originally a client of hers, you see."

Of course I knew that. It made sense that as he used natural remedies before he met his wife, that he would continue to do so.

"Did the Chinese herbs work on his driver?"

William smiled. "Yes, I believe they did, not to the extent where he could still drive, mind you, but Colin Greaves said it brought the man significant relief. He still had to rest up, but he wasn't in the terrible state he would have been in otherwise."

"It sounds like you were quite friendly with Mr. Greaves."

William frowned, or more like scowled. "Not really. We were amicable enough, but he was putting considerable pressure on us to sell." His face brightened and he added, "But he did buy products from us every time he came here to try to force us to sell the shop."

"And you said he didn't ever threaten you?"

William shook his head. "Not explicitly, although he made it clear enough that it wouldn't be good for us if we didn't sell to him. He always said it in a joking manner, but he made it clear that it was no joke."

"If you had to hazard a guess, who would you say murdered him?"

William scratched his head. "I'm completely

stumped on that one. It couldn't have been his driver because he had a migraine that day."

I thanked him and left. I headed back to my sister's store, discouraged. William had not given me any useful information, and I still had no idea who had killed Colin Greaves. One thing was for certain—I had to figure it out in a hurry before the police arrested me.

When I reached the apartment, I unlocked the apartment door and had opened it ever so slightly when a gray and white streak ran between my legs.

"Oh no!" I cried, as Mr. Crumbles ran away as fast as he could, his tail fanned out. I pulled the door shut, locked it, and took off after him. I sprinted around the corner straight into a hard body, and recoiled in horror.

It was the man who had been following me.

CHAPTER 22

"I'll scream if you don't get away from me," I told him, trying to sound brave, though I heard my voice quivering.

I was trembling.

"I don't want to hurt you, Mrs. Delight," he said.

"Miss," I said automatically. "The police know you're following me. Why have you been following me? Do you intend to murder me too?" My voice broke.

His eyebrows shot skyward. "Murder? Of course not." He reached into his coat pocket. I gasped and backed up, my palms pressed into the cold brick wall.

Instead of a gun, he pulled out a card and

handed it to me. "I'm a private investigator," he said.

I looked at the card. On it was written:

Arthur Cole, Private Investigator. Cheap rates. No job is too small or too big.

I was a little concerned that the card was printed on awfully thin paper and looked unprofessional, although maybe he just had a low budget.

"Did my husband pay you to follow me?" I asked him. "Does he think I'm going to get a lawyer and contest the pre-nup?"

Arthur Cole frowned so hard his brows formed a unibrow. "I'm afraid I don't know what you're talking about."

"Don't play dumb with me," I said, gaining a little courage now that I knew he was a private investigator rather than someone sent to harm me. "Then who paid you to follow me if it wasn't my husband?"

"I thought that was obvious," he said, scratching his head. "Colin Greaves."

"Colin Greaves sent you to follow me?" I said. "But he's dead."

"I was paid in advance," he said, nodding as he spoke.

"But then who do you report your information to since Greaves is dead?"

"Obviously, the person or persons who have taken over his business still want the information," he said, "and they shall remain nameless."

"What could Colin Greaves have possibly wanted to know about me?" I said. "I don't own the store. I mean, surely it was because he was trying to buy the store from my sister? The store is owned by my sister and her husband. It's got nothing to do with me. How would investigating me help Mr. Greaves?"

He shrugged. An air of indifference clung to him, as did the unpleasant smell of stale cigarette smoke and some sort of alcohol, maybe gin. "I only do what I'm told to do. Mr. Greaves wanted you investigated as well as your sister. You're non-Amish, so he thought you might be influencing her not to sell."

"I don't understand," I said. "What could you possibly find out about me that would have made my sister sell the store to him?" I could feel a headache coming on. This wasn't making much sense. If only Matilda was here to make sense of it all, but she would probably simply quote Miss Marple.

Arthur Cole spoke in a slow drawl. "He thought he might find out a piece of juicy information about you too that he could use to encourage your sister to sell the store."

I thought that over. Slowly, it dawned on me. "Oh, I see. If you found out I was running from the law or something like that, Colin Greaves could have blackmailed my sister to sell the store to him. Otherwise, he'd give that knowledge to the police."

Cole fixed his eyes on me. "You're not as silly as you look, Mrs. Delight."

"Just call me Jane," I said. I was weary from correcting everyone to 'Miss'. "Well then, what did you find out about me?"

He made a guttural sound. "Only about your boring marriage. No offense intended."

"None taken," I said. "And of course you would never find anything bad about my sister since she is Amish."

"I wasn't really expecting to find out anything about your sister, nor was Greaves," he said. "It was the others he wanted to know about."

Something occurred to me. "Hang on a moment. You said you wanted to get some dirt on me *too*. Does that mean you found something incriminating about someone else?"

"I'm sure I didn't say that," he said.

I jabbed my finger at him. "You most certainly did. You said *too*."

His face flushed beet red. "You're mistaken."

I waited a while, but he said nothing more. "Do you intend to keep following me?"

"That's privileged information," he said, "but I haven't been able to find anything about you. Following you hasn't turned up anything at all, and I will be reporting that back to my employers."

"Let me guess," I said. "Stephanie and her son, Brooks."

"You know I can't tell you," he said.

I put my hands on my hips and gave him my best stare, to no avail.

"Well, I'll be on my way. Good day to you, Mrs. Delight."

With that, he turned away and slipped back into the shadows. It was then I remembered I was looking for Mr. Crumbles. It was certainly not safe for the little cat to be out.

"Mr. Crumbles!" I called, followed by "Here, kitty, kitty, kitty," in pleading tones.

I walked around for another five or so minutes trying to find him. I finally spotted him heading in the direction of William and Mia's store. From a distance, I saw Mia leave with another lady, and before the store door shut, I saw Mr. Crumbles slip inside. I called out and waved my arms at Mia, but she didn't hear or see me.

I ran as fast as I could to the store and was out of breath by the time I got there. Maybe I really should start working out. William was in the process of shutting the door as I burst through. He shut it behind me and flipped the sign to Closed. "Jane," he said. "We're closed for the day. Is there anything I can do for you?" Irritation was stamped all over his face.

"I'm terribly sorry, but my roommates' cat just ran in here," I said. "I saw your wife leave with another lady and the cat slipped in. I called out, but she didn't see me."

William pursed his lips. "Cats? I don't like cats. Pets are nothing but a nuisance and they are a waste of money. Besides, what will the health inspector do if he catches the cat in my store?"

"I'm so terribly sorry," I said. "I would have caught him by now only that private detective delayed me."

William suddenly froze to the spot. "What do you mean?"

"You know, that private detective who Colin Greaves sent to spy on us?"

William's whole demeanor changed. His eyes narrowed into slits. "Are you trying to be funny, Jane?"

"Not at all," I said, indignant. "I had no idea who he was and I'd even called the police about him. It's just I actually ran into him then—I mean literally ran into him. I ran around the corner, looking for the cat, and ran straight into this man. He gave me his card. It said he was a private detective. He said he'd been looking for dirt on both of us."

William took a step toward me and I took a step backward. He was suddenly menacing somehow.

"What do you know?" he said. He took a step to the side and pulled down the blind over the front window. "Are you trying to blackmail me too?"

"Of course not!" I said. "I am certainly not the sort of person to blackmail anyone. Besides, I don't know what I could possibly blackmail you over."

"Look, I'm not known for my patience," William snapped. "You said you called out to my wife when your cat got in and she didn't see you? Are you quite sure?"

"Yes, of course I'm sure," I said.

"And you expect me to believe this story?"

"It's the truth."

William Willow certainly was behaving strangely and I had no idea why. I wondered if he had a drinking problem, or maybe all the stress had gotten to him.

He reached out for me, his long bony fingers digging into my shoulder. "Stop playing games. Tell me what you want from me."

"I don't want anything from you. I just want to find my cat." I said the words slowly but loudly.

He loomed over me. "How much do you want?"

At that moment, the realization hit me. He thought I wanted to blackmail him.

Suddenly, inspiration hit me. "Greaves was blackmailing you, wasn't he!" I regretted the words as soon as they were out of my mouth.

"Yes he was, as you no doubt found out from that interfering private detective. Greaves was blackmailing me all right. I was involved in a crime some years ago, a bank robbery to be precise, and I was the police informant. I left town and changed my name, and Greaves found out and said if I didn't sell him the store at a cheap price, he would tell the criminals where I was."

"Couldn't you have gone to the police?" I asked.

"Of course not," William snapped, his face turning an unpleasant shade of red. "I did a few other illegal things that wouldn't be good for the police to know about. Greaves found out about them as well. My wife doesn't know and I can't let her find out. She would be devastated and would probably leave me. That's why I had to kill Greaves. I didn't want to, but I had no other option. I'm sure you understand that."

I didn't understand at all. I wondered if he was going to lunge at me. He was a large man with broad shoulders. I looked around for a weapon. Maybe I could grab one of the glass jars and hit him with it. My cell phone was in my purse, but I wouldn't have time to get it out and call anyone. Cold fear coursed through my body.

William was still speaking. "Greaves was a nasty man. A very nasty man."

"But how did you get the poison into him?" I said. I was curious, in spite of the dangerous situation in which I found myself.

"I knew he was due to come that day," he said. "I told my wife that when Greaves came the next time, that she should leave the shop and I would close it, because I wanted to speak to him in private.

She readily agreed and wasn't at all suspicious—why would she be? I knew your sister put out samples of cupcakes, so I put out a plate of savory cupcakes. I filled them all with wolfsbane. I got rid of them all afterwards. I knew Greaves was heading straight to your sister's store after he left mine."

"Were you trying to frame my sister?" I asked him.

He looked surprised. "Of course not! Anyway, it worked. Now what am I going to do with you?"

I backed away from him. "Well, I won't tell anyone. Actually, I'm surprised the private detective hasn't told the police that Greaves was blackmailing you because then they would know you had a motive."

William snorted rudely. "He isn't really a private detective who is on the level," he said. "He's a criminal who was doing some work for Greaves, that's all. He can hardly go to the police, and in fact I'm sure the police would like to get their hands on him."

"But, but he gave me his card," I sputtered.

William rolled his eyes.

I wondered if Matilda had ever been as naïve and gullible as I was. I sure had a lot to learn about sleuthing.

"I'm glad my wife didn't see you," he said. His fingers tightened once more around my shoulder.

"My roommates and sister know I'm here," I said. It wasn't true of course, but I didn't know what else to say.

It all happened quickly. One minute William Willow had me by my shoulders and I was scared he was going to strangle me. Next thing I knew there was a loud crash. He collapsed, unconscious, to the ground.

I looked at the ground to see broken glass. It took me a few moments to realize that a large glass bottle had broken over his head.

Mr. Crumbles nimbly jumped down from a high shelf and walked around my legs, purring loudly. I picked him up and hugged him. "Thank you, Mr. Crumbles," I said. I then deposited him back on the ground and called the police, doing my best to stop my hands from shaking.

CHAPTER 23

We were all sitting in the apartment. Rebecca had closed the store early to celebrate with us. Everyone was fawning over Mr. Crumbles, and he was certainly enjoying the attention. I had bought him a tin of sardines and a little packet of cat treats. I had also bought him his own set of keys to play with.

Eleanor had made Mr. Crumbles a birthday cake from layers of canned cat food.

Matilda pointed to the cake. "Why are there two candles on that cake? That cat isn't even a year old."

Eleanor's cheeks puffed up. "A cake needs candles, and we don't know his age."

"But it's not his birthday," Matilda protested.

"How do we know? Anyway, it's a reward cake, not a birthday cake."

Matilda looked quite put out and opened her mouth to say something, but quickly shut it. I expected she was going to point out that reward cakes are not likely to have candles, but thought the better of it.

"He's a very clever cat," Eleanor continued, "dropping that glass jar right on the murderer's head before Mr. Willow could do Jane any harm."

"Nonsense!" Matilda snorted. "The cat didn't know what he was doing. He always knocks things off high shelves and he just happened to knock it onto the murderer's head. It was all a coincidence."

"It wasn't a coincidence at all," Rebecca said. "I have been praying for Jane's safety. It was the Lord who saved her."

"God saved her by means of Mr. Crumbles, of course." Eleanor pulled a face at Matilda. "Mr. Crumbles was just like Moses, when God used him to part the Red Sea."

Matilda was clearly furious. "What on earth are you talking about! Have you completely lost your mind, Eleanor?"

"Saved by the bell!" I exclaimed as the bell to the apartment rang. I made to stand, but Mr.

Crumbles took a big leap onto my lap and purred. He sounded like a freight train.

"I'll get it," Eleanor said. She soon returned with Detective McCloud.

"I'm glad to see you're all right, Jane," he said by way of greeting.

Matilda leaned over to me. "When did you become Jane and not Miss Delight?" she asked in a stage whisper, causing my cheeks to burn.

"William Willow has been charged and I've come to take you downtown to give your witness statement, but only if you feel up to it now," Detective McCloud said.

"I just need some more coffee and another chocolate or five before I feel ready to drive down there," I told him.

"I'll give you a ride," he said, which made Eleanor and Matilda giggle, much to my embarrassment.

"Have you found that private detective yet?" Rebecca asked Detective McCloud.

He shook his head. "No, not yet, but I'll have Miss Delight look through some mugshots, if that's all right?"

"Sure," I said, a little disappointed I had been

demoted from Jane to Miss Delight. "I'm just glad it's all over."

"Yes, it is all over," McCloud said. "And you're not in any danger from that private detective even though he isn't licensed and was working for Greaves."

"Have a seat, Detective," Matilda said. "Jane has a few more chocolates to eat before she'll be ready."

Eleanor walked back in from the kitchen—I had not noticed her leave—and set a steaming mug of coffee in front of the detective. She offered him a chocolate cupcake, which he declined.

"All's well that ends well," Matilda said.

"Is that a quote from Agatha Christie?" Eleanor said.

"No silly, it's obviously from Shakespeare," Matilda said snarkily.

Eleanor pulled a face. "I know that. I was being sarcastic. You usually only quote Agatha Christie. It can be quite bothersome at times."

I looked at the bickering sisters and could not help but chuckle. All truly had ended well. We were all safe, and my sister got to keep her store with no more threats from Colin Greaves. And despite the fact that my husband was now married to a much younger woman, I didn't mind any more. I had my own life now. I had the company of my sister and two rather quirky, elderly women who had already become my friends. I was sitting in their company with a delightful cat and a rather handsome detective. What more could I want?

Jane, Matilda, and Eleanor—plus Mr. Crumbles!—are back in the next book in this USA Today Bestselling series: Previous Confections

THE LAST THING Jane expected was to meet Cherri, her ex-husband's new wife, but that's exactly what happens.

It's bad enough that Jane's Amish sister has a broken arm, so Jane has to run the cupcake store with dubious help from feisty octogenarians Matilda and Eleanor, and naughty little cat, Mr. Crumbles . . . but Cherri wants Jane's help in solving a murder.

Will Jane be able to solve the murder, avoid her ex-husband, keep the cupcake store from crumbling apart, and keep a level head around Detective Damon McCloud?

Or will it all end not so sweetly?

AMISH RECIPE

SHOO-FLY PIE

Shoo-fly pie (wet bottom) *Melassich Riwwelkuche*

Ingredients

1 cup flour
2/3 cup brown sugar, firmly packed
1 tablespoon vegetable shortening
1 egg

6 fluid ounces molasses
6 fluid ounces boiling water
1 teaspoon baking soda
1 9 inch unbaked pastry shell
1/4 tsp each of Ginger, Cinnamon, Cloves and Nutmeg

Method

Combine the flour, brown sugar, and shortening.

Set aside 1/2 cup of this mixture for the topping.

Add the egg, molasses, boiling water, and baking soda to the remaining mixture.

Spread this mixture into the un-baked pie shell.

Spread half cup of crumb topping over the pie.

Bake at 375°F for 10 minutes.

Reduce temperature to 350°F and bake for 30 minutes or until firm.

Crumbs

Ingredients

1 1/2 cups all-purpose flour
1/2 cup brown sugar
2 tablespoons butter or vegetable shortening

Method

In a medium bowl, combine flour, brown sugar, and butter or shortening. Rub with fingers to form fine crumbs. Set aside.

Preheat oven to 375 degrees F (190 degrees C).

Pie crust

Ingredients

4 cups all-purpose flour

1 tablespoon granulated sugar

1 1/2teaspoons salt

1 1/2 cups butter or vegetable shortening, cubed

1 egg

1 tablespoon vinegar

1/2 cup water

Method

In the bowl of a food processor, pulse the flour, sugar, and salt until combined. Add butter or shortening.

Pulse until pea-sized crumbs form.

Place dough in a large bowl. Bring the dough together with a wooden spoon.

Whisk together the egg, vinegar, and water in

small bowl. Pour over the dough and mix until combined it sticky dough.

Cover with plastic wrap and chill in the refrigerator for at least 1 hour before rolling.

Place oven rack on the lowest. Preheat oven to 375°F.

Halve the chilled dough in half on floured surface.

Roll half of the dough to ¼-inch thick and place in a 9-inch pie dish.

Loosely fit aluminum foil over the lined pie dish and weigh down with pie weights, or uncooked rice. Bake for 25 to 30 minutes. Remove the weights and foil and continue baking for 10 to 12 minutes until golden brown.

Chocolate Whoopie Pies

Chocolate Cake

Ingredients

2 cups sugar

1 cup oil

2 eggs

4 cups flour

1 cup dry cocoa

1 tsp salt

1 cup sour milk or buttermilk

2 tsp. vanilla

2 tsp. baking soda

1 cup hot water

Filling

2 egg whites, beaten

4 cups confectioners sugar

1 tsp. vanilla

1 1/2 cups vegetable shortening

Method
Cake

Combine sugar, oil and eggs in large mixing bowl. Beat until creamy. Sift together flour, dry cocoa and salt. Add dry ingredients to creamed mixture alternately with sour milk or buttermilk. Stir in vanilla.

In separate bowl, whisk baking soda and hot

water together until soda is dissolved. Stir into batter until thoroughly mixed.

Drop by rounded spoonfuls of desired size onto well greased baking sheets. Bake at 350 degrees for 8-10 minutes, or until top springs back when touched. (For moist Whoopie Pies, avoid over baking.)

Remove from sheets and allow to cool completely. Spread filling on flat side of one cookie and top with another. Wrap completed Whoopie Pies individually in Saran Wrap.

Filling

Beat egg whites until stiff. Add sugar, vanilla, vegetable shortening.

Beat until smooth and fluffy.

Fill cookies as above.

ABOUT RUTH HARTZLER

 USA Today Bestselling author, Ruth Hartzler, spends her days writing, walking her dog, and thinking of ways to murder somebody. That's because Ruth writes cozy mysteries.

Ruth is also is known for her Amish Romance novels as well as archeological adventures, for which she relies upon her former career as a college professor of ancient languages and Biblical history.

www.ruthhartzler.com
Click on the following image code to be taken to the website

ABOUT RUTH HARTZLER

Made in United States
North Haven, CT
27 December 2024

63559736R00167